The Darkness Within

Also by Jaime Rush

A Perfect Darkness
Out of the Darkness
Touching Darkness
Burning Darkness
Beyond the Darkness

and coming soon
Darkness Becomes Her

The Darkness Within

A Novella

JAIME RUSH

EPub Edition MARCH 2012 ISBN: 9780062121431

Print Edition ISBN: 9780062184603

10 9 8 7 6 5 4

The Darkness Within

Chapter One

"The male victim, according to witnesses, was torn apart and gutted like an animal."

That line from the newscast drew Tucker Cane to the television, where the reporter shoved the microphone at a police officer and asked for more details.

"It looks like a wild animal attack, maybe wolf or panther. We can't comment until we know more. For now, we advise residents of the Las Vegas suburbs not to wander into the desert areas after dark and to be on alert."

From what Tucker could see in the churning red and blue colors and spotlights, the area looked like a typical suburban neighborhood.

A woman with tangled hair and wild eyes pushed her way in front of the camera. "It wasn't no wild animal! I saw it. The man that did this turned into smoke, and then a werewolf! I told the police, but they won't listen. The monsters are going to get us all!"

An officer took the woman by the arms and led her away as she struggled and continued to rant.

Every hair on the back of Tucker's neck stood on end. He glanced to the kitchen and then the stairs going up. He already knew none of the Desert Rats—the D'Rats—were home yet. Their cars had been absent from their various places in the driveway when he'd come home fifteen minutes earlier. He'd turned on the news and gone into the kitchen to grab a beer.

In the seven years since he'd found those who were like him, gathered them and cobbled together their ragtag family, Tucker was as close to a parental unit as they'd ever had. Not that he tried to be. What did he know about taking care of someone? He was only twenty-four, and he'd hardly had a parental role model himself. He did, however, know firsthand how shocking it was to discover how different you were, and the reason you had the skills you did.

He rewound the newscast to the part he'd missed while he'd been in the kitchen, and watched from the beginning. The attack had occurred three hours earlier, the victim identified only as a male in his twenties. Apparently this had been news for a while now. They had already spoken with a biologist called to the scene, trying to determine what kind of animal would commit this act and how the fine citizens of Las Vegas could avoid being next.

Typical hype, but the attack didn't sound typical.

The biologist squinted in the light. "We haven't seen an animal attack like this since a local man who was mauled twenty-three years ago, also in a residential area."

"What kind of animal was responsible for that attack?"

"We couldn't make a determination due to lack of evidence. We found no fur or distinguishable prints in the sand outside the house. The only thing we found, at both scenes, were bloody prints that *appear* to be paw prints. In this investigation, it's still too early to rule out anything."

The hairs on Tucker's arms now joined the rest at attention. The man who was mauled back then was Del's father. Supposedly Tucker's father had killed him in a fit of jealousy.

Del. Damn, the thought of her cut into his chest even now. He finished half his beer in one long pull, pacing the living room. It hit Tuck then: the victim was a male in his twenties. He started calling the D'Rats . One was on his way home; the other, on a date. Tuck told them to get their asses home, now.

The door banged open, and Darius wheeled inside. He'd been with them only three years, the newest member of the family. Tucker still didn't feel as though he knew him. The dude had been paralyzed in a car accident right before Tucker had found him. He wore his hair in a wavy, poufed style that reminded Tucker of a fifties 'do.

Darius spun his fancy new chair around and kicked the door closed. He grunted, obviously the only greeting he was going to give Tucker as he headed to his room.

"Been running?" Tucker let those words hang, taking in the sheen of sweat on Darius's face, the damp hair at his neck.

Darius paused at the beginning of the hallway. "Yeah. Moon's not up until three."

Dark enough to camouflage him.

Tucker waved him over. "Come here. You need to see this."

He played the newscast and watched Darius's expression darken when the woman broke in with her hysterical account. Tucker paused at the end of the segment.

"We knew there might be others out there like us. The men responsible for what we are—our biological *fathers*—liked to visit prostitutes. Stands to reason our mothers weren't the only ones who got pregnant."

"I think it was a wild animal, and that that crazy broad reads too many vampire and werewolf novels . . . with her heroin."

Tucker shook his head. "She said the guy turned to smoke first. That's not something any werewolf or vampire I've ever heard about does."

Darius wheeled down the hall to his room and shut the door with his usual kick. It always sounded like an angry slam.

Tucker had heard that sound enough as a child.

He called the one female in their group and asked her to come over. Time for a meeting. He paced, hoping the others would come home soon. He supposed this was how parents might feel—worrying about their kids—as the tightness coiled around his chest. But it wasn't only their safety that had him knotted up. What they harbored inside could render any of them mad, vicious . . . uncontrollable. He knew it only as Darkness. Either there was another person out there with it . . . or one of the D'Rats had gone mad. That was the possibility he feared most.

ELGIN WATCHED THE newscast in his boss's office, his mouth growing tighter with each revelation.

Torus looked just as grim. "You see why I called you in. Sounds like Darkness."

Elgin nodded. "It wasn't me or the others. We were playing Dead Man's Poker when it happened."

"My son was here last night. So likely it wasn't one of ours, which means we have a larger problem. How long has it been since you and the others were doing the other kind of poking?"

Elgin's shoulders grew rigid but he answered the question in a neutral voice. "Twenty-five years or so. You're thinking it's one of our offspring?"

"I would hate to think you had offspring. Is that possible? I want you to think back to when you went into Vegas and availed yourself of the pleasures there. I know you well remember the consequences of your actions. But there may be bigger consequences, ones that could expose us." He walked in front of Elgin, assessing him with sharp, gray eyes. "When you had sex with those women, did you use protection?"

"I put on a condom," Elgin said, his chin lifted, eyes staring just past Torus.

"Did you keep it on?"

Elgin mouth tightened. "No. I had a way of slipping it off during the act. Otherwise it felt artificial, like getting yourself off while wearing a glove. We can't contract the humans' diseases, so it seemed safe enough."

"Did you think about pregnancy?"

"Those women wouldn't lose their livelihood by having a baby."

Torus slapped Elgin across the face. Elgin jerked from the impact but kept his expression passive, his posture respectful. He could Become, take out the man right there. Torus didn't hold Darkness, but he had powers of his own. A mutiny would have further consequences.

"Taking the chance was foolish. We know Darkness can be passed on to offspring. Did the other two do the same?"

After a moment, Elgin nodded.

"Could you find those women again?"

"They're probably no longer in the business."

"If you sired a child who inherited Darkness, he or she would have no idea what it is that lurks inside them. One false move, one deception, and they become a beast. Perhaps in front of others, as was the case tonight. It presents a huge problem, one that started with you . . . and must end with you."

Elgin swallowed hard. "We'll track down the women. If there are any children, there won't be many."

"That should make your job easier. Get Bengle and go now. I'll free up the other one from his duties and send him out. You must use your senses. Scour the city for anyone in their early twenties with our vibration."

"What do we do when we find them?" Elgin asked.

"You each have skills for taking out someone quickly

and quietly. They will have no idea what you are, so you have surprise on your side. Make it look like an ordinary street crime. If they were raised in that environment, they won't be far from it." Torus's eyes narrowed. "Your former wife is dead, correct? You assured me of that when you went berserk and killed her lover."

Torus's recrimination was clear in his voice. He'd almost killed Elgin for that, but he'd suffered greatly for breaking the rule—and losing control.

Elgin nodded. "I took care of her body so it would not be found."

"You said that, yes. Don't let us find her alive, Elgin. It will be over for you."

Chapter Two

Del handed the dark-haired boy in the chair across from her a stuffed bear. "Tucker, I want you to pretend that whatever has happened to you has also happened to this bear. What would you say to him? What would you do to comfort him?"

The boy frowned. "My name's Taylor."

Del blinked. "Of course, it is."

"You called me Tucker."

She flopped back in her chair, mentally replaying what she'd said. Then she covered her face in shame. "I did, didn't I? I'm so sorry, Taylor." She pulled her hand away and met his guarded gaze. "It's just that you remind me of a boy I once cared very much about, and his name was—is—Tucker." Could she have felt any smaller? Well, yeah. "Can you forgive me, sweetheart?"

The endearment had slipped out. She hadn't gotten to the endearment phase with Taylor yet. She was really blowing it with this kid. A kid who looked like another lost boy with the ability to tug at her heart.

The boy shifted his blue eyes to the bear, and then slowly, heartbreakingly, he started pounding on the bear's face. This was the hard part, having to stuff her outrage and grief so the children wouldn't see it.

"Who does that to you?" she asked in a carefully modulated voice.

He told her, haltingly, and she took notes while keeping her fingers from tightening into fists.

After his foster mother came to take him, Del took a deep breath and held the bear to her chest. Everything the boy had told her flashed into her mind in pounding blasts of images and feelings. She gasped at what he hadn't told her, the parts too dark to share with a stranger who couldn't even get his name right.

She stumbled to her desk and typed in the notes she couldn't share because she could tell no one how she'd come by them. Her skills helped her, though, to draw the truth from the children she saw at the Family Service Center. They could dump out all of that ugliness, and she could protect them. She knew what it was like to hold in secrets, though she'd never endured what these children had.

Tears slid down her cheeks as she translated what she'd seen, what that poor boy had suffered. *Pull it back. You can't fall in the pit.*

"Del."

She jerked at the sound of her mother's voice. "Mom. What are you doing here?" When she took in her mother's pale face, she jumped to her feet and met her as she staggered into the small office. "What's wrong?"

"Can you get to the internet from your computer?" Carrie asked, closing the door.

Del's stomach dropped. "What is it? Did something happen?"

Carrie leaned against the desk. "Go to Thirteen Action News's web site. There's a story."

Del brought a chair around and guided her mom into it, then pulled up the web site. Under the *TOP STORIES* banner was a frozen newscast, titled, *Man mauled in mysterious animal attack*. With her throat dry, Del clicked on the arrow to play the footage.

The reporter stood in front of a house with yellow tape strung out around the perimeter. "This morning we're standing in front of a crime scene unlike most others. The victim, twenty-nine-year-old Fred Callahan, was found last night, mauled by what appears to be a wild animal. What makes it unusual? Investigators have found no evidence of an animal. One eyewitness told police a harrowing story." They played a clip from the night before of a woman screaming about werewolves. "That woman, whose name has not been released, is the only witness. The police are reluctant to connect this death with the mysterious mauling death of Tony Stevens twenty-three years ago, but an unidentified source confirms the details of both cases are identical."

Whimpering sounds came from Carrie's throat. Del reached for her hand. Tony Stevens. Del's father, who had died before she was born.

Del rubbed her mom's back. Fortunately, she couldn't pick up emotions or energy from people. She had, of course, felt the leftover energy from her mother's grief and guilt over the years, and wished she could erase it somehow.

Carrie wiped her eyes. "One of them murdered that man, just like Elgin murdered Tony."

One of *them*. The people she'd come here with, who had settled in northern Vegas. Carrie had come as a wife, not involved with the energy resources project they were here for.

"You think it was Elgin?"

Carrie started to nod but paused. "Elgin broke the rules, risked exposing the group when he attacked Tony. For all I know, he was executed for it. Torus, the group's leader, kept a tight rein on us. We even lived in one neighborhood. I doubt that's changed. So maybe it wasn't one of the men who held Darkness. But it can be passed on to any children they might sire." She looked at Del. "Like the boy my former husband sired. He has Elgin's Darkness, Del. He could have—"

"No, it wasn't Tucker."

"You don't know that."

Del stood, releasing her mother's hand. "I do know. Tucker lived with us for four years, Mom. I *knew* him. Beneath that street-smart exterior he had a good heart. Maybe if you hadn't sent him away—"

"Maybe if *you* hadn't given in to your damned hormones." Carrie stood too, her voice sharpening, face contorting in anger. "I took that kid in off the streets as soon as I recognized he was Elgin's offspring, gave him a home. You were the one who made me send him away." She jabbed a finger at Del. "I told you not to get romantic with him. Then I walk in and find the two of you . . ." She shook her head, making her blond, fine hair fly out to the side. "So don't you dare put that guilt trip on me. I've got enough to carry."

Del put her hand to her chest to ease the pain. It had been more than hormones. So much more.

"I'm going to work." Carrie stood, and her prickly energy wilted. She brushed a stray hair from Del's face. "I'm sorry, sweetheart. I loved Tucker, too, but I couldn't take the chance of him going crazy and hurting you. I don't know what Darkness is, other than something like black magic. What I do know is that it makes a man violently possessive of what he considers his." She paused to drive that point home. "Someday when you're in a relationship with a nice, normal man, you'll see I did what was for the best."

Del backed away from her touch. "How can I be with a nice, normal guy, Mom? I'm not normal."

Carrie let out a soft sigh. "When you find the right guy, he'll accept you as you are. It will happen, if you'll just start dating. Stop comparing every guy who's interested in you to Tucker."

Del's eyes widened. "I don't—"

"Yes, you do. The first boy you fell for was gorgeous, haunted, and had a dangerous edge. I know he kept doing the street cons and that he was pulling you in, too. We'll talk later."

Del didn't confirm or deny either allegation. While she had tried to reform Tucker's penchant for making money by gambling, he *had* managed to draw her in, seducing her with the excitement and risk. But that she compared the men she met to him . . . ridiculous.

She watched the news video again after her mother left. That one of them was out there, killing, made her very uneasy.

Chapter Three

WHEN DEL'S PHONE dinged that afternoon, indicating a text message, she saw first that it was from her mother. Then three more messages came in bursts. Each one stole Del's breath.

Stay away from the house.

Do not report me missing.

I think they found me.

It's time for me to go back.

They. Her mother had warned that if her people ever found her, Del had to be careful. If they somehow discovered Del's existence, they wouldn't like that someone with their DNA was loose among the population. They might even kill her. Carrie was sure they were unhappy about her being out there. Sending her back to her dimension was the best-case punishment for running away.

"No. No." The words tore from a throat so tight, it was a wonder any sound could emerge.

Tom, one of her fellow caseworkers, peered into her office. "You okay?"

She leapt from her desk. "I have to go. My mom . . ."

"Go. I'll make sure your appointments are rescheduled."

She thought she smiled in thanks but couldn't be sure. It was probably more like a grimace. She was at a full-out run by the time she reached the parking lot. The cool air smacked her in the face, but hot prickles kept her from feeling the lack of a jacket. She drove to her mother's place of work and had to keep herself from racing into the austere law firm.

"Goodness, girl, you look like you ran all the way here," the receptionist said.

Del could only imagine that her hair was disheveled, clothes damp and wrinkled. "Is Mom here?" Her desk was unoccupied.

"She hasn't come back from lunch yet. She had a window of about twenty minutes to eat, poor thing, before she was due back for a meeting." Tammy checked her watch. "Hmm. She's late. That's not like her. You know your mom. She's the most responsible person I know."

Del had to choke back a sob at those words. "Do you know where she went?"

"She usually grabs lunch from one of those carts; God knows what's in their food." Her expression became concerned. "Maybe she got food poisoning."

Del dashed out, having spotted two of those carts as she'd come in. She asked the vendors if they'd seen a woman of her mom's description.

"Oh, yeah, nice lady. She was here about twenty, thirty minutes ago," one man said as he filled a taco for a customer. "She went that way."

Del followed where the Hispanic man pointed, searching everywhere. Maybe she was hiding and would spot Del. She found a courtyard, the secluded kind of place her mother would seek out. She walked to one of the benches and ran her fingers along the wood slats. A barrage of feelings hit her like a cold wave of water: a murmur of a kiss, an argument about money, both muted from the wood. Nothing as dramatic as fear.

She tried another bench and sensed her mother's energy here . . . and yes, fear. Del flattened her palm against the wood. Hard to get a sense of what had frightened her. Just like with electricity, wood didn't conduct feelings or imprints well.

She sank onto the bench and pulled out her phone, hoping for a new message. Taking a chance, she sent her mom a text back, just a question mark.

The *ding* her mom's phone made when it received a text message sounded from a short distance away, though slightly muffled. Del sent another text, a period this time. The sound chimed again. Her heart tightening, she sent more texts and followed the sounds to a garbage can. Baffled, she took off the lid and started digging, fighting nausea at the smell of food and stale coffee.

She found the phone with the pink cover, and fear vibrated from it. Still no images to go with it. Her mom had ditched her phone. She would only do that if the situation was dire, to keep someone from looking at her contacts, especially the entry for her daughter.

I think they found me.

Cold waves washed over her body. She couldn't notify the police. Who could she call for help?

Tuck.

The name reverberated in her mind as clearly as the emotions she picked up from objects.

Her first thought: he wouldn't help her. Clearly he'd pushed her into the black box in his heart where he buried all the terrible things that had happened to him. Her mother would engender no warm feelings either.

She wrapped her arms around herself. Tucker was the only person who knew who *they* were, who understood the danger. She had to find him, at the least to tell him there might be trouble.

She drove into the area of the city where she'd found him a year ago, near the Strip. She'd been on her way to one of the casino hotels for a quick visit with a birth parent who was trying to get her act together. A crowd on the sidewalk *oohing* and *ahhing* over something in the center of the circle they'd formed wasn't unusual, but she was drawn to it anyway.

That something turned out to be Tucker, dressed in a tight black shirt and pants, performing tricks of illusion. He'd learned to use his particular skills to earn money—not conning but entertaining.

When he'd moved in with her and her mother, he'd been a thirteen-year-old con artist. He conned her right out of her heart. Her mom, too. Four years later, one kiss changed everything.

She pulled into a parking spot, but her mind was back in that moment seven years ago. It was as vivid as though it had happened last week . . .

Del and Tuck burst into the house, laughing so hard they were clutching their stomachs.

"Do you think he's figured it out yet?" Tuck asked, falling back against the wall while trying to catch his breath.

"Probably not. God, did he deserve that. He's been ripping off kids for years."

Tuck pulled out a wad of mangled bills from his jeans pocket. "Here, take half. Take it all, I don't care. You were brilliant."

She took the wad, knowing that his offering it all to her was a great honor. His early years of hoarding every scrap of food or penny to survive were ingrained in his cells. She threw the bills into the air, and they rained down over them. Which started them laughing again.

Tuck hadn't laughed much during the first years he'd come to live with them, implicitly following the rules as though he expected her mother to change her mind and send him away. Carrie's biggest rule: they were not to get romantically involved. The idea seemed preposterous at first, but as they'd grown older, she'd started to become ultra-aware of him. She'd caught his gaze lingering on her at times, too, a spark of hunger in his eyes.

Now Tuck's eyes lit with mirth; his mouth curved with it, carving dimples in his cheeks. She knew he was gorgeous, but seeing him all the time, she'd gotten used to it. Now . . . oh, now, it hit her all over—the way his face had become lean, his chin square, his muscles defined and shoulders broader.

She and Tuck shared a bond with the psychic skills that made them different from everyone else; now that she was sixteen and he, seventeen, their bond centered on how he used his skills to pull cons.

Their laughter faded by degrees as she realized she was staring at him, and he was returning that stare, eyes heavy, smoky.

His gaze dropped to her mouth, and she knew he was going to kiss her. Suddenly any bit of excitement from a con paled to the flutter of her heart, like a dozen finches released inside. She licked her lips as he moved closer. She met him halfway, and everything changed.

He pulled her against his body, his hands sliding through her hair, tilting her head for a perfect angle. His tongue knocked at the door of her lips, slid in when she parted them, and moved languidly through her mouth.

His body gave away his desire, and that stepped up her already racing heartbeat. He wanted her, that's what that hard ridge pressing against her stomach told her.

His hands moved down her arms, to her sides, thumbs brushing the curves of her small breasts. She leaned into him, rubbing her pelvis against his . . . My God, she'd done that to him, made him hard. She wanted him, too, and the forbidden lure, the thought of going *there* washed over her like hot, thick honey.

"You don't know how long I've wanted to do this," he said, his voice low and rich.

"Me, too," she said between kisses.

Vaguely she heard the sound, one she realized later was the door opening. But Tuck's mouth was on her ear, his breath hot and moist, and then on her neck, so she didn't give it much thought because her mom wasn't due back for an hour—

"What are you doing?"

They both lurched at the screeched words. Her mom stood at the door, looking shocked and betrayed.

"Mom . . ."

Carrie threw her purse down, sending a tube of lipstick and a pen skittering across the floor. "No. You are not doing this."

He stood rigid, hands clasped in front of him. "We haven't done anything."

"Yet. If I hadn't come home, you sure as hell would have."

"Miss Carrie, I know you don't want us involved, and I tried, I did. But Del's an amazing girl. She—"

Carrie's gaze had dropped to the bills on the floor. "What's this?" She pinned him with furious eyes. "You're still gambling. And you, Del . . . you're doing it with him, aren't you?"

"She was trying to talk me out of it," Tuck said.

Carrie's anger morphed to sadness, resignation, and somehow that alarmed Del more than the anger. "I should have known. Put a boy and a girl together, throw in hormones . . ."

He'd called her amazing. The word echoed, warming the coldness that gripped her. "Mom, Tucker's special.

Okay, he gambles, but only with jerks who deserve to lose their money. This is the first time we've done this. Any of it."

"It'll be the last."

"Why? You're always saying what a great kid he is, how far he's come. He is great. And I like him. A lot."

Carrie took them in. "Sit down."

Was she going to give them the talk? Use condoms, be responsible. Wasn't that what she was worried about?

They sat next to each other, but a respectable distance apart.

Carrie sank wearily to the chair across from them. "I need to tell you both something. I've been putting it off, but it's time. Past time." She clasped her hands together. "You're not like the other kids. You know that. You both have abilities. Gifts, I called them. But they are not gifts; they're curses. Not because of what they are, but where they came from."

She twined her fingers, staring at them for a moment before looking at them. "Have you heard of string theory, quantum physics? There are respected scientists who believe in other dimensions, worlds that exist side by side with this one. I'm from one of those other dimensions. Tuck, so is your father. We are human; at least that's the theory. But centuries ago, our people descended far below the surface. The Earth's magnetic energy changed us. It gave us a different body consistency, and the ability to manipulate energy. Or read it. Both of you hold the essence of a Callorian. That's what we're called."

Carrie turned to Tuck. "When I met you, I knew you

had Callorian blood. We can feel each other, like the vibration of a strong electrical current. I also suspected your father is my former husband, Elgin. You have his eyes and facial structure. He would go to the casinos and find the prostitutes who worked there. I'd rather he go to other women for that. Callorians have no feelings, or at least we are taught to bury them. But some of the people who came here hold an energy called Darkness. Elgin didn't have it when we married; he came by it later. I don't know what it is; he wouldn't tell me, only that he'd tapped into a powerful energy source and he now 'held Darkness.'"

She made finger quotes. "It changed him, turning him from a cold man to one with too much passion. He became possessive, territorial, and volatile. He lost his temper once and became a beast. That's what Darkness does, he said. Allows you to change your energy to become something else. Something of your choosing."

Carrie rubbed her arms, and seeing that she had their attention, disbelieving and shocked as it was, continued. "I was afraid of him, so I left, changing my appearance and name and hiding in Vegas. I met Tony, Del's father, and fell in love. But Elgin came after me because I was his. Tony tried to fight him, but he didn't know . . ." Her voice broke. "I hadn't told him yet, afraid to lose him. Especially since I was pregnant. He only knew my husband was violent. I ran, thinking Tony was behind me. But he stayed behind to fight Elgin, who became a beast and tore him apart."

Del knew about that part, but not about her mother's ex becoming a beast.

Carrie turned her teary gaze to Tucker. "You hold Darkness. I can feel it in you as I felt it in him, a peculiar heaviness. I know you would never intentionally harm Del. I have seen your friendship grow, your protective nature. That's one of the marks of Darkness. You will kill to protect her. That would be hard enough on her. But if you thought she was cheating, you might kill her. You wouldn't mean to, but it would overtake you."

He was shaking his head. "No. This is crazy."

"I wish it was." Carrie shook her head, her expression one of genuine agony. "But think about it: you've always felt different. You have abilities no one else has. And haven't you sensed something dark inside you?"

The dreams. Tucker had confided recurrent nightmares about turning into a beast.

Carrie said, "Hold out your hand. Focus on an animal you admire. Think of its paw."

He held out his hand, fingers splayed. Nothing happened.

"Now, think of Del kissing another boy."

His eyes narrowed as he concentrated, then widened as a shadow surrounded his hand. With claws. He jerked his hand back and shook it, as though it were on fire. It looked normal again.

Carrie shuddered, turning away. "I'm sorry, but you had to know sometime. Better now, before you accidentally Become and expose yourself. People would think you demonic. They would kill you. You have to do everything you can to keep your abilities, and Darkness, hidden. You don't want to hurt Del, do you?"

"No. Hell, no."

Carrie looked as though she were going to cry. "I'm so sorry, Tucker, but you have to go. You and Del have crossed the line, one I know can never be uncrossed."

"Del." That word, filled with agony, drew her attention from his hand. "Del, look at me."

Fear kept her from meeting his gaze. She could not reconcile the beast her mother had just told her about with the man sitting beside her.

"No, Mom. I don't believe it!" Not Tucker. He could never possess the evil that had killed her father.

Carrie sighed. "See for yourself. Get your father's ring."

The ring Del wasn't allowed to touch, for fear she would experience the end of her father's life. Del ran to her mother's room, flipping open the old jewelry box. Del pulled the ring from the box. She needed to see it for herself.

The images hit her: a man who looked like Tucker stalking toward him. "She's mine," he growled, the words soaked in possessiveness. In front of her, his body morphed to a smoky substance, and then formed into something not human, not animal. It vaguely resembled a lion, made of black oil.

Her father's fear and confusion rocked her, her mother's screams for Tony to run. But the sight of the unholy beast froze him, and Elgin lunged. She felt the claws tear into Tony's neck, the warm blood gushing down his chest and spraying across the floor. Pain and fear rocked her. She dropped the ring with a gasp and dashed to her mother's bathroom, retching in the toilet.

Her stomach kept heaving until nothing more came up. She washed her face and rinsed her mouth, startled at the pale but blotchy girl staring back from the mirror. Weak, wasted, she stumbled back out. Tucker's bedroom door was half open, and she pushed it. He wasn't in there.

"Where's Tucker?" she asked when she walked to the living room and didn't see him there.

"He's gone," Carrie said, staring at the door.

Del ran to it, but her mother grabbed her around the waist. "Let him go, Del."

She fought, calling out his name, but she was so weak. Her mother's arms were like iron clamps, and finally Del sank to the floor and cried.

She went to school the next day, unsure whether he'd be there. The school year was nearly over, and Tucker hadn't been overly fond of going anyway. At P.E. she spotted him on the other side of the chain link fence that divided the different areas. He was looking at her with an expression of desolation. She couldn't stop herself from leaving the track where she was running laps, drawn as always to him.

He met her there, his fingers curled around the fence wire. "You turned away from me . . . ran away."

She shook her head. "I had to see what my mother had described. It was horrible. I got sick. You were gone when I came out. Where did you go? Where did you sleep last night?"

"Mrs. Markham's house. She's visiting her kids, so I slept on her couch." He held out his other hand, long fingers, nails trimmed. "Look. Nothing. No shadow or paw or whatever it was. Maybe it was some optical illusion, because we expected to see something. I tried all night, Del. I tried to Become something. It didn't work. She's wrong. Your mom is wrong." Desperation permeated his voice. "She's just freaked out, or maybe she's crazy. You heard what she said. 'Another dimension'? That's insane. Right?"

He laughed, the sound hollow. "She kicked me out. I did nothing but kiss you and she kicked me out. Del, you have to get out of there. She might see some shadow in you, too, and kick you out. What will you do then? Leave with me. Tonight."

His order shot panic into her. "I can't just leave my mother. Yeah, she's paranoid, and kicking you out was an overreaction, but if you'd seen my father being murdered"—she swallowed hard, remembering those wild gray eyes, so much like Tuck's—"you'd understand. I touched his ring and experienced everything that happened in those last minutes of his life. I had to see for myself, because I didn't believe her."

"And you believe her now?"

Del nodded. "Your father morphed into a beast, just like she said."

He winced. "Don't look at me like that. Like it was me, like I'd do something so terrible. Maybe she made you see it. Like she made us see the paw." He reached through the fence and gripped her wrist. "Come with me, Del. You're mine."

She's mine. She heard that man's possessive statement in Tucker's words and, with a yelp, jerked her hand away. "Did you hear yourself?"

He took a step back, his expression shell-shocked. "I didn't mean it . . . like that."

Her mother's words echoed: *You wouldn't mean to, but it would overtake you.*

"We didn't imagine it," Del said, tears in her voice and in her eyes. "We can't pretend it didn't happen."

She wanted to. Oh, how she wanted to go back to when it was just her and Tucker, and she knew nothing of desire or Darkness or death. But she couldn't erase the images. The truth burned in her mind, a relentless recital of her father's pain and fear and murder.

He shook his head. "No. We can't." He strode to the back edge of the fence where it was shorter, and launched over it, tearing off down the street. A coach yelled after him, but Tucker never stopped.

She clutched her hands to her chest. "Tuck." The word came out a whisper. She touched the metal where his hand had been. His pain rocked her so hard it threw her head back. She let out a small cry and sank to her knees, because twined with his love for her was that fierce possessiveness she'd heard in his voice. He was as dangerous as her mother had said.

Yes, she was afraid of him. Afraid of what was in him. But in the days after that, she desperately needed to see him again. He wasn't at graduation, wasn't at Mrs. Markham's house, wasn't anywhere. She'd sneaked out late at night for weeks, taking her mother's car and driving around the areas she knew he'd grown up in. He'd disappeared, taking her heart with him.

Then, when she'd least expected it, she found him a year ago. He'd been the one who turned away from her. She had gotten a taste of what he'd probably felt, and God, it hurt. Even worse, she'd seen nothing in his slate gray eyes when he looked at her. No emotion or longing, only cold disregard. She wasn't expecting a warmer reception now.

And what if he's the one who killed that guy?

She'd told her mom she knew Tuck would never do such a thing. In truth, she didn't know him, not anymore. Seven years had passed, seven years of God-knew-what. But he was all she had.

Chapter Four

Street performers and cons usually carved out their turf, or so Tucker had told Del. He made a circuit, going from spot to spot within his turf so that by the time he returned, there would be a fresh crop of tourists.

The February air nipped at her cheeks as she walked from her car to where she had seen him last. The sky was brilliant blue with clouds that looked like frosting spread too thin. The cold didn't keep the tourists and gamblers away. The end of the world probably wouldn't keep them from Vegas.

There was a new breed of street performer: people in costumes who would pose with you in a photo opp for tips. She passed on offers from Mickey Mouse and Batman.

"I live here," she growled as Captain Jack Sparrow approached.

Tuck wasn't at the place where she'd found him before,

so she kept searching. She felt cold from the inside out, even beneath her heavy coat.

The sound of applause down a side street twenty minutes later drew her attention. Yes, a group of people gathered, their breath puffs of fog that hung in the air. A rock song from the eighties played in the background.

She heard his voice first, low and smooth with a hint of the theatrical. The crowd was quiet between bursts of applause. They formed a tight circle around him, but Del managed to nudge her way in.

Even after his rebuff, the sight of him clutched at her stomach. He wore the black pants and shirt, opened just enough to show the tan V of his muscular chest. His sleeves were rolled up, hands moving gracefully as he unraveled what looked like a coil of black rope. It reared up, as though to strike the man in front of him, and he jumped back. The "snake" evaporated, and the crowd applauded.

Sunlight reflected off Tuck's dark hair, long enough to brush his collar. He turned to an attractive woman at his side. "And madam, what is your heart's desire?"

"You," she said on a laugh, not entirely kidding.

He bowed, one arm pressed against his stomach. "That may be arranged. But what can I make for you in front of these lovely people?"

Her cheeks flushed. "A rose."

As he came up from the bow, he held a rose made of the same black substance as the rope. He extended it to her, and the moment she reached for it, the rose also evaporated. He gave her a conciliatory smile and shrug. "Ah, isn't love fleeting?"

He'd always had beautiful hands. While Del was looking at those hands, he suddenly turned and speared her with a look. He'd known she was there last time, too. Did he have that ability to sense others that her mother had spoken of?

All thoughts fled, though, as she felt the impact of those icy gray eyes, and then their quick dismissal. It was a stupid idea, going to him. She wasn't even sure what he could do, but she would go crazy if she didn't talk to someone.

He threw up handfuls of what looked like black dust, and as it rained down on him, he disappeared. Literally disappeared. A moment later, he reappeared with a flourish of his arms. The crowd applauded wildly.

It hit her. He wasn't using his telekinesis. *He was using Darkness. As a trick!*

He bowed, signaling the end of the show, and thanked everyone for their kind attention. People tossed bills into a carved wooden box until it nearly overflowed. He stood nearby, watching it with one eye as he spoke with the last of the crowd.

"You're as good as any of those boys at the big casinos," one man said, dropping a twenty into the box.

Tucker leaned down to tweak a knob on the iPod speaker system that supplied the music. "That would be too much like working for someone, but thank you, sir."

The woman he'd made the rose for handed him a bill inside a folded piece of paper and whispered something. He wrapped his fingers over hers, gave her a sultry smile, and kissed the back of her hand. She might have stayed, but she glanced over at Del, who was clearly waiting to speak with the great magician. She murmured something to him and walked away, leaving just Del. Just Tucker.

The group singing from the iPod chanted about "Wild Boys," but Tucker looked all business, closing the box with a *snap* and placing it into a suitcase. He kept his back to her, his pants pulling tight across his ass with his movements. He was more filled out in the shoulders now, still slim in his hips, more . . . grown-up. Not the boy with the soulful eyes who'd realized he'd claimed her.

The memory of those words shivered through her.

He yanked up the handle of his suitcase, his back to her, ready to walk away. "Next show is in an hour."

"You know I'm not here to watch your show."

He tilted his head back, as though looking at the sky. "You should go."

All she could say, the only word she could get out among the many crowding into her mouth, was, "Tuck."

He spun around, his eyes no longer dull with apathy. "It's Tucker. Or Mr. Black to people I don't know."

She took a step forward when she wanted to back away. But no, the anger sparking in his eyes was a good thing. He hadn't shut her out. Not completely.

"Mr. Black? Your stage name? Sounds . . . appropriate."

She needed to ease in. Blurting out that the woman who had kicked him out was missing wasn't going to engender his help. If it could be engendered.

"Thanks for your approval." The spark disappeared, and he turned to leave again.

She pushed herself forward, touching his upper arm. It was hard, solid.

He jerked away. "You cannot seriously be wanting to talk, to chat, to catch up on old times."

"I wanted to do that last time. I wanted to tell you how sorry I was, how awful I felt, but you shut me out." Emotion leaked into her words, baring her pain and sincerity.

His mouth tightened. "Because I had nothing to say to you, and that hasn't changed. Try again in, oh, five more years."

She had to grab his arm before he turned away again. "Tucker, please. I need—"

"You *need*?" He laughed, a harsh sound, nothing like the last time she'd heard him laugh. "You need something from me—am I getting that right?"

No, this wasn't going to be easy at all.

"I need to talk to you."

He leaned into her face, the scent of mint on his breath. "Well, we talked, sweetheart. And it was *really* nice. As nice as the last time we talked, seven years ago when you ran off as your mother was kicking me out." He slapped his hand over his chest, making a hollow *thump*. "Warms me right here. Gotta go."

He might as well have thumped her chest, too. Her fingers clenched as he walked away with that confident gait. She knew he wouldn't look back, just like last time.

"They took my mother!" she called out.

He kept going.

She had nothing to lose. "*They*. You know who I'm talking about. They came here and grabbed her or somehow made her go with them." She had to call out louder as he walked farther away. All the fear and agony she'd managed to stuff behind a calm façade spilled into her voice. "They're here, wandering around Vegas. I don't know who else to talk to. No one but you knows . . ." She let the rest drift away, unwilling to scream out about their freakhood. He turned the corner. "I need . . ." It hit her then, washing over her, warbling *you, Tucker* into a sob.

She sank to the sidewalk, her legs weak, and tried desperately to get herself under control. No, she didn't need Tucker. She would figure this out herself. She wiped at her eyes and got to her feet. There wasn't time for grief, fear, or self-pity. Dumb idea to appeal to Tucker. But at least she'd warned him.

"What happened?"

She started at the male voice right behind her, spinning to find Tucker. He'd flatly asked the question, as though some part of him felt obligated to query. His eyes looked just as flat, even framed by the thick, dark lashes she'd envied so.

Her heart jumped. *He's just listening. It doesn't mean anything.*

"I got a series of text messages from her." She dug in her purse and extracted the phone. After waking the screen, she handed it to him, not trusting herself to read them aloud.

He took the phone, his eyes narrowing as he read.

"They," she said. "It has to be the people she came here with. Maybe even her husband. Your biological father."

"She says it's time to go back. Maybe she went willingly." He held out the phone to her.

"No, she'd never do that." She took it, afraid he'd dismiss her concerns. "She'd never leave me like this."

"People change their minds. They leave. They disregard you, throw you away. Happens all the time."

Damn, he knew exactly what to say to plunge a knife into her and leave her defenseless.

"I'm sorry you felt that way. It hurt me, too."

His laugh was harsh. "Yeah, while you had your mother and a roof and food. You probably hurt for a few minutes."

And now twist the knife.

"I was sixteen, Tucker. *Sixteen.* And what you are"—she glanced around as people passed by, lowering her voice—"scared me. I saw that beast. And when you said 'You're mine,' it was the same way Elgin had said my mother was his, right before he killed my father."

He pulled her into his arms, slamming her against his body. "You're not sixteen anymore. Still afraid of me?"

She pushed him away. "Stop. That's not fair."

"So the answer is yes." His voice lowered, eyes flashing with devilment. "As well you should be." He held his hands aloft, flexing his fingers like claws. "Who's afraid of the big bad wolf?"

"Don't be an asshole." The word shocked her, coming out as it did. She needed a tame vocabulary in her line of work, even if worse words than that applied to some of the parents. "You're using it, aren't you?" He was obviously comfortable with what he was now. Even, she guessed, enjoyed it. "You're using Darkness in your act." The words came out as a hiss.

"I don't *eat* people in my act." He stepped close again, running his fingers down her neck, gently drawing his nails across her skin. "I don't tear out anyone's throat. So don't take that haughty tone with me. I've made peace with the cards I've been dealt."

His fingers had drawn down to the top of her collarbone, leaving a trail of heat and tingles. She grabbed that hand but found she couldn't let go. "You like holding Darkness."

His eyes flicked to where she gripped his hand before meeting her gaze again. "It's part of me. I've mastered it. Never once has it taken me over." He moved so close she could feel that minty breath on her jaw, feel the brush of his barely-there stubble when his chin brushed hers. "Do you want to know what I Become, Delaney?" he whispered.

She shoved him back. "Stop. If you don't want to give me any suggestions on how to find my mother, fine. I get that. I hurt you, and no matter how many times I say I'm sorry, it will never, ever make it better. So punish me by walking away. Don't punish me by trying to scare me."

He jammed his fingers into his front pockets, tilting his head. "You knew I still held Darkness. It's not something I'm going to outgrow. Why did you come to me, of all people?"

She knew she was outsmarted, out . . . *somethinged*. No matter what she said, it wouldn't go over well. Being honest was all she could be. "Because you're the only one who understands. You were the only one who came to mind." She released a ragged breath. "I know. We were all *you* had once. My mother kicked you out, and you thought I turned away from you." She gestured, waving him away. "So go. You can have that satisfaction again."

He didn't turn, though. He seemed to consider her. Probably he was enjoying her pain. He would never believe how much she'd suffered, too, so there was no need to tell him now.

He gripped the handle of his suitcase, fingers flexing over the handle. "Come."

The word hung in the air, incongruous with the fact that he was indeed walking away.

Had she heard him correctly? Maybe he'd said *Go on*, and she'd look like an idiot following him.

So she stood, her throat so tight she thought it might shatter if she swallowed.

He paused, turned, and gave her a questioning look. "Having second thoughts?"

And third and fourth, but the question loosened the grip her confusion had on her. Relief flowed now, weakening her bones. She shook her head and joined him.

She wanted to cry, to gush gratitude, but she stuffed everything and walked silently beside him. To where, she had no idea.

He led her to a parking garage, and then to an old sports car. She'd never even heard of a Datsun. He popped the hatch and tossed the suitcase in the back with a practiced move.

She didn't wait for an invitation, getting in on the passenger side when he opened the driver's door. Closed inside, his energy seemed to throb, pulsing through her. He started the car and turned up the heat. The interior was immaculate, the stereo a high-end brand. The rock music pouring from the speakers made it feel like she was at a concert.

His gaze remained ahead as he blindly turned down the volume. "Tell me what happened."

"How are you?"

She wanted to know what he'd done when he left the schoolyard, how he'd survived. She'd comforted herself with the fact that he'd been basically living on the streets when they'd found him so he knew how to take care of himself. He'd never talked about what had propelled him from the shabby apartment he shared with his mother.

He turned to her at last, impatience in the lines around his mouth. "This is about your mother, not me. Not us."

"She loved you, Tucker. It hurt her, too, but she was so afraid. Not crazy, but crazy-afraid."

"Don't." He shook his head, gripping the gearshift. "I don't want to talk about the past. There's nothing there for me. We talk about what happened today or we don't talk at all."

"Okay." She told him everything, which was damned little.

He crooked his fingers. For a moment, she thought he was gesturing for her to come closer. Her body wanted to lean toward him, but she realized he meant for her to give him the phone again.

He read through the texts. “She sent them in short bursts because she wasn’t sure how much longer she would have a chance to warn you. She doesn’t want you to go to her house, because she thinks they might have been watching her, maybe traced her there.” He glanced at her. “Still the same place?”

She nodded, and he turned away for a second. To hide his reaction to the memories?

“There are pictures of you there, papers, records. Evidence that you exist.”

“Yes, I suppose.”

“Tell me everything you know about the people we’re the offspring of. Why did they come here? Carrie didn’t exactly give me a lot of information before she tossed me out on my ass.”

“She tried to find you, you know. The next day. She knew she’d reacted out of fear and motherly instinct, and she wanted to talk to you, give you some money.”

“Motherly instinct. Yeah, she didn’t want me eating her daughter.” His mouth quirked. “In any way.”

Del’s cheeks flushed at the implication.

“I didn’t need her money,” he said. “But more knowledge would have been nice. I had enough to get by, as it turned out.” He waited, apparently not going to tell her what he’d had enough for. “Carrie said something about the people who came here from the other dimension. Why were they here? How many?”

“She never told me much either, other than their people had come here to study our energy resources. She didn’t say how many had come, but I gathered there was a group of them. They settled here, keeping to themselves but living as normally as possible. Mom wasn't even sure they were still here . . . until that attack last night. But it's damned strange that someone with Darkness killed that man, and the next day my mom goes missing. She told us she left her people, but in reality, she ran away. After so many years, she figured they weren't looking for her anymore."

He ran his hand over his hair as he absorbed what she was saying. "We have to figure out why they took her. Why now? You're right. Seems unlikely that one of them would happen onto her the day after the attack."

This was why she needed him. He was detached—well, mostly detached—and could see it from a position that wasn't soaked in fear. Because he had no emotional investment in the outcome of her mother's fate.

"Mom didn't think it was one of them who killed that man. The penalty for potentially exposing the group is pretty severe. It's why she isn't sure Elgin, her former husband, is even still alive."

A shadow passed over his face. "Wait a minute. You don't think I—"

"I wouldn't be here if I thought you . . ." She couldn't say the words. "She thought it could be anyone those men with Darkness sired." She put her hand on his, wishing she could read his feelings. "I told her you weren't capable of doing something like that."

"You don't know me at all." He let those heavy words settle.

She pulled her hand back, and he moved his out of reach, clamping onto the steering wheel. "I know you have a good heart, Tucker. I do know that."

He shook his head. "No, I don't. For a while I believed that. For a few short years, I felt worthwhile. You and your mom gave me that. Then she told me I was some uncontrollable beast who would harm her daughter, and kicked me out of your lives. So you know where my heart is?" He gestured to the suitcase. "Performing. Making money."

She saw him at the fence again, and it tore at her heart. But she'd said she was sorry and it had meant nothing, so she swallowed the words. "I'll pay you to help me."

He gave her a scornful look. "Who said I'd help you at all?"

"You're making this so hard." Yeah, it had come out a bit whiny. She cleared her throat. "Please help me. I've got some money in my savings. It doesn't have to be about our past. Treat me like a stranger. I know you can do that."

He blinked at that accusation. "I don't want your money."

She'd seen the box filled with cash. No, he didn't. He certainly didn't need her or her trouble. "Thanks for listening." She opened the car door and made to leave.

"Get back in the car, Del."

She paused, debating whether to make her stand and leave, or see what he had to say. She sank back into the seat and yanked the door closed. Pride had nothing on helping her mother.

"We'll go to your mom's house, see if anyone's been there. If they haven't, we'll remove anything that suggests she has a daughter."

He started the car. The engine roared to life, obviously not the original engine. It sounded like a racecar. He turned up the stereo, backed out, and headed out of the garage.

Okay, I get it. You don't want to talk on the way. Fine.

His taste in music in the car ran more to modern, though she didn't recognize the alternative rock song. An angry-sounding guy was singing about it being his last resort.

When Tucker lurched onto the street, she grabbed for something, anything. Her hand closed over the gearshift before his hand came down over hers to shift it.

In that second, she felt what he'd felt when he gripped it in frustration: his pain and his irritation at it. Anger. And she heard his words echoing: *You don't know me at all.*

Chapter Five

What the hell are you doing, Tuck? You don't need this. You definitely don't damned need her.

He glanced surreptitiously at Del, now clutching the seat belt strap. He needed to vent, and taking corners fast was helping.

No, it wasn't.

He turned up the next song, *Something to Die For* by the Sounds and tried to focus on the way to the house, far from the glitz of the Strip. It would bring back memories, both good and bad. He'd put his attention on the bad.

He sank into darker thoughts, the implication of her mother's disappearance the day after the attack. And the fact that having Del sitting there in his passenger seat coiled through his chest in a way he didn't like at all.

Awhile later, he turned into the old neighborhood, trying not to feel anything. He hadn't returned here since the day after Carrie kicked him out. No drive-bys, no stalking or anything. He'd shut the door on that part of his past and moved on.

He was, after all, the beast Carrie had said he was. Over those next few days he'd tried to Become and failed, nearly convinced she was bat-shit crazy. Then he did, feeling his body change, feeling the energy of what he was morph into something entirely different.

He never let himself get involved with any one woman long enough to see if he would feel murderously possessive. Women were nothing but trouble anyway, and while he loved partaking in carnal pleasures with one every now and then, that was the only use he had for them. Like that luscious bit at his last show.

Except he was looking at Del, with her long, dark brown hair and the brown-green eyes that had haunted his dreams for a long time. She glanced up at him, those eyes now filled with worry and other things he didn't care to identify.

She turned away, her fingers tightening on the strap even though he wasn't driving like a madman now. She pointed to the house on the right. "You passed it."

He studied the door and windows as he drove past. No sign of anyone inside. "We're not going to park in the driveway."

"In case they come while we're here. Of course." She put her hand over her mouth. "God. This is not real. It's a nightmare." She pinched her arm, her thigh, then looked at him.

"Am I often part of your nightmares?" he asked.

"No." She tucked a strand of hair behind her ear. "Thank you, Tu— Mr. Black."

Yeah, he'd been an asshole back there. It had come as a shock to feel something when he'd seen her standing there. The last time he'd been able to shut her out, as well as any lingering emotions. He had to remind himself she'd only come to him because she needed his help.

But she hadn't the last time she tried to talk to you.

He paused in front of a house with a *FOR SALE* sign in the yard. Mrs. Markham's house. "Does she still live here?" He'd taken a big risk when he'd broken into her house all those years ago. He hadn't taken anything, just slept on her couch and ate some cereal, but he could have been arrested for trespassing.

"She recently moved in with her daughter in Phoenix. It's vacant."

He pulled into the driveway, cut the engine, and got out. He scanned the neighborhood, which was quiet during the workday. Kids played down the street; a car passed by, the driver not paying them any mind. Giving her a nod to follow, Tucker walked to the back yard and followed a fence that separated several of the houses here to give them privacy. Someone might spot them cutting through their yard, but he and Del would already be gone before they could be questioned.

He was paying as much attention to his senses as he was to his vision. Unfortunately, if he felt the tremor of someone like him, they would feel him, too. Still, it was better than being taken off guard. Of course, he was feeling Del's tremor, like the stinging tentacles of a jellyfish, which might distract him from picking up someone else's tremor.

He slowed as he approached Carrie's house. He remembered this little backyard, had spent many an hour kicking around a soccer ball with the kids in the neighborhood. And a few evenings sitting on the back steps talking to Del about school, life, anything but the raging desire he'd suddenly developed for her along with his facial hair and morning wood.

He pulled her close to him as he leaned at the edge of the window and peered inside. No sign of movement.

She held up a key and gestured to the back door. He nodded, and she slid it in and quietly turned the knob. She stepped in before he could nudge her aside and go first. So he shadowed her, searching the dim kitchen where they'd come in. No sign of disturbance. He stepped in front of her and walked to the living room. His body froze, and he instinctively grabbed her arm.

She sucked in a breath at the mess. The drawers in the desk were upended on the floor, files and papers scattered everywhere. Before he could stop her, she dashed to Carrie's bedroom, her hands gripping the doorframe. There was no sign of chaos here, nor that Carrie had packed anything.

He pulled Del along, checking the rest of the house. "They're gone."

She dropped to her knees, picking up her mother's open wallet. "This is how they knew where she lived." She looked at the papers. "But what were they looking for?"

"You, probably. They'd want to know if she had children." His chest tightened. "She would die before she'd reveal you." He'd never known that fierce kind of motherly love, but he'd been a threat to one who felt that way about her daughter.

Del gasped, a choked cry.

He reached for her before thinking better. It was her despair that had drawn him back earlier. He had a weak spot for genuine tears.

Or maybe you have a weakness for Del.

No. That ship had sailed, that heart had shattered. He settled his fingers on her elbow, guiding her to her feet. He looked at the wall where once there had been school pictures of Del—and of him, too. Two pictures were missing. "Were your pictures hanging there?"

Her fearful eyes took in the wall with the two bare hooks. She nodded.

"Please tell me she didn't have any of me. No, she didn't," he added when he saw her contrite expression. "It's a good thing. We'd better go. Is there anything your mother would have in there with your address? Any information about you?"

She looked lost as she took in the papers on the floor. "I don't know, I don't know." She knelt again, picking up a card. Her fingers trembled as she turned it over: a mother's day card. "I mailed this to her, and I know she kept all her cards in their envelopes so she'd have the dates."

The envelope was missing.

"Did you put your return address on it?" he asked.

She nodded. Del was now a target. An inconvenience,

probably. That old protectiveness reared up. "We're going to your place, because that's where they're going. And that may be our last chance to find her."

DEL FOLLOWED TUCKER along the same route back to his car. She didn't question him, even though she could safely talk. He'd survived on the streets, knew how to elude muggers or perhaps even the police.

Once they were back on the road, she directed him to an apartment complex not far away. He cruised the parking lot, surveying their surroundings with narrowed eyes.

"What are you looking for?" she asked.

"Your mother. The guy who grabbed her might have subdued her and left her in a car so he could go up and take care of you."

A whimper escaped her throat. Her mother, knocked out, tied up, possibly in a trunk. Some guy hunting her down.

"Can you sense me?" he asked.

She blinked at his question. "What do you mean?"

"The reason I knew you were in the crowd was because I felt you. Do you feel the tremor when you're with me?"

How could she begin to sort out what she felt when she was with him? "I feel something, but not as distinct as that."

His face was a mask of concentration. She searched, looking for a man who might be the kind of person who would kidnap her mother.

The moment she saw the big broad-shouldered man step out from the courtyard entrance, Tucker's hand flattened against her face and he pushed her down to his thigh.

"He's one of them," he said. "He's looking for you."

She stared over his leg to the dashboard, fighting an urge to look, because she'd gotten a flash of dark hair and silver eyes . . . Tucker's father. His hand remained, keeping her in place.

"Shhh," he said softly.

She felt the car turn, heard him slide down his window.

A man's voice floated on the air. "Bengle, it's Elgin. Where are you? . . . Found any of your little bastards running around yet? . . . Me, either. We just need to find the one who went berserk and we'll be done with it. I need your help. I've got an old problem I've got to take care of. I—"

The sound of a car door closing shut off any further words they might hear. She lurched up, pressing close to Tucker to stay out of sight. A green Buick backed out of the parking spot. She searched for any sign of her mother in the car. He was alone, or appeared to be.

"Elgin," she said. "That's the man my mom thought was your father. He looks just like you."

"Yeah. He does." Tucker closed the window and backed out, too. "He didn't pick up on us, which could mean your mother is in that car. If he felt a tremor and didn't see us, he'd assume it was hers."

Del imagined her lying in the back seat . . . or, more likely, stuffed in the trunk. She stared at it, two cars ahead of them, as though she could see straight through the metal. She couldn't, of course, and forced herself to settle back in her seat. Tucker looked casual, slouched in his seat, one hand draped on the wheel. But his gaze was on that car, too.

"What are we going to do?" she asked, gripping the seat belt with fear and frustration.

"We follow him."

"He called Mom an 'old problem.' I'm sure he was talking about her. If Darkness makes you territorial, he must have been furious that she left him." She ran her fingers across the seat belt. "Have you ever felt it?"

"No."

She looked at his profile, the jaw that gave away his tension. "What he said . . ."

"I know. He's looking for his bastard children. Because they think one of us killed that man. We're a liability, just like you are."

"The man he was talking to, he's obviously looking for his offspring, too."

His expression froze. He picked up his cell phone and dialed as he cut through traffic, remaining three car lengths behind the Buick. "We have another problem. Our daddy's in town . . . yeah, *that* daddy. And he's not alone. Apparently they're looking for their bastards. I'm guessing it's not for a warm reunion." He gave a description of the man and his car. "Call the others and put them on alert, tell them to meet at the house. I'll be home in a bit."

He disconnected, set his phone into the center console, and didn't offer any more information about that call.

"Who was that?" she finally asked, because sitting there watching the ass-end of the Buick, with her mother possibly locked in the trunk, was about to drive her crazy.

"Greer. My brother."

That socked her in the chest. "You have a brother?"

"Half-sib. Same father. We think so, anyway." Tucker took a corner, nice and easy. "We have the same eyes." He swallowed hard, making his Adam's apple bob. "That man's eyes. Otherwise we look nothing alike. His mother was Apache, and he took after her."

She imagined a man with Native American looks and gray eyes. "And there are others?"

"Yes."

She wasn't sure if he was unwilling to talk about them or if he was concentrating. She let him concentrate as they wound their way north. His life was none of her business anyway. The sun was beginning to sink behind the mountains.

She started worrying the seat belt again. "What if he's taking her to this compound where they all live?"

"When we get away from traffic, I'm going to run him off the road. Be ready to pop the trunk, grab your mom, and get her out of there. Take his car if you can. If you can't, take mine."

"What about you?"

"I'm going to distract the guy, and if I can, take him out."

" 'Take him out.' You mean kill him?"

His fingers curled around the steering wheel. "I don't mean take him out for dinner, Del."

"No need to get smart-assed about it. It's not like I'm used to hearing someone say they're going to kill another person."

"In my world, sometimes it's kill or be killed. You have to be ready to defend your life, because there are plenty who will take it for a buck. Or a fu—" He clamped his mouth shut. "You get the idea."

God, she did. She didn't want to imagine his life, but that gave her a brutal picture. "Have you ever killed someone? I mean, could you do it?"

"Yes. I killed a guy who was trying to rape this boy." He flicked a glance at her, and she had to wipe the horror at the thought of that from her face, because she knew why that would tear him apart. "I killed him with my human hands. Took his knife and cut his throat. I made the world one sleazeball better." He nodded to the car ahead. "And I have no problem doing it again."

She looked away from him. She was no stranger to the vulgarities of life and how ugly people could be, but she'd never talked to someone who had killed before.

Isn't that why you came to Tucker? Because you knew he was capable of doing what needed to be done?

She stilled that inner voice and kept her eye on the green car.

Traffic was still heavy, workers fleeing the city while others drove in for the evening. Tucker stayed back, hopefully far enough that Elgin wouldn't pick up their vibration.

"Have you been working on the skill we used when we pulled that con?" Tucker asked.

"No. I wasn't as good as you were. Psychometry is enough."

"I could always tell when you were lying, Del. Remember that."

She wrinkled her nose. "I play with it, when I'm bored. I can move papers and pens on my desk. I close my door sometimes. But that's when I'm not scared or stressed out."

"What do you do for a living?"

"I work with kids at risk. I'm a caseworker for the state."

He slid her a look. "I bet your psychometry helps with your job."

"It does. I give a child a bear to squeeze while I ask them questions. Then I take it and see what they're not telling me. Not that I can use what I pick up in court, but I can sometimes coax the child into telling me the truth."

She thought about the boy she'd just met with. The one with Tucker's eyes.

He gave her an appraising look. "That suits you. You were always about saving some poor kid or another. I remember you defending the underdogs at school when they were being picked on. That first time you saw me, I could see your compassion as you made a beeline right for me. I didn't know what compassion was at the time, but it felt good."

She smiled at his admission. "I could see that you were a wounded child. But it was more than that with you. I could probably feel the tremor on a subconscious level."

"Did you ever use your ability to see my past?"

She thought about lying but decided against it for more than one reason. "Yes. I didn't mean to, but we lived in the same house. It was hard not to touch what you touched."

"What did you see?"

"It was the harshest thing I'd ever seen in my young life. I saw your mother hit you for walking in while she was conducting . . . business." She shifted her gaze away. "I saw her trying to talk you into letting this creepy guy touch you, because he would pay a lot of money for that. I felt your anger at her betrayal, your shock." She forced herself to look at him, but his expression was shuttered. "That's why you ran away, isn't it?"

"Yeah. I wasn't going along with that."

She let out a long sigh. "I wish I could take away all those terrible memories. That kind of ability would definitely be a gift."

She held out her fingers inches from the pair of red dice hanging from the rearview mirror. Real dice, not fuzzy ones. He wanted to know if she could help fight, if necessary. If she could move something. It didn't come as naturally to her as it seemed to for Tucker.

The dice didn't move, other than with the natural sway of the car's motion. He was watching her, his expression unreadable. Leaving Tucker to spirit her mom away, if it came to that, didn't feel right. It felt like losing him all over again, but this time there'd be some guy trying to tear him apart.

God, she couldn't think about that. "Talk to me."

"About what?"

"I don't know. Sitting here unable to do anything, I feel like I'm going to explode."

After a moment, he said, "I find it hard to believe you're sitting there at all."

"Me, too."

"I've thought about you a lot over the years."

Those words washed over her like warm honey over a chilled body. "Then why did you turn away from me when I saw you last year?"

"I didn't say they were good thoughts."

Pain rippled through her, but his words weren't harsh. "You could have yelled at me, told me what a terrible person I was." Anything was better than being dismissed. Maybe he knew that.

"I ignored you because I didn't want to go back there. It wasn't only that you ran off right after your mother dumped that news on me. It was what happened when we talked by the fence."

"You were the one who ran off then."

"Because you looked at me like I would hurt you." Now his words weren't so matter-of-fact.

"I could feel your Darkness. You wanted me to run away with you. You said I was yours, and the way you said it scared me."

He was silent for a moment, his eyes on the road ahead. "It scared me, too. It's why I left."

She released a breath, and with it, the self-hatred she'd felt for so long. It wasn't all her fault. "I had just seen the images of Elgin when he found my mother and Tony. The way Elgin said 'You're mine' right before he killed my father . . . you said it the same way. I could understand why my mother lives in fear of them, of Elgin. Even of you. It was horrible, vicious, and my mom suffers from the guilt of it every day." She looked over at him. "But that's in the past now. Maybe we can—"

"No maybes. We can't be friends or anything else. I'll help you, but that's where it ends . . ."

"So why *are* you helping me?" Dumb. He might rethink it, change his mind.

"You and your mom took me in for a while. No matter how it ended, I was safe and well fed. I always repay my debts."

"Thank you for helping me, whatever your motivation."

She flipped her hand toward the dice, and this time they swung away from her. He gave her a nod of approval, which made her feel stupidly proud. So she made a face at him.

He didn't respond, other than a tightening of his fingers over the wheel. He had moved on; why couldn't she?

Because she had been trying to make it up to Tucker with every kid she helped. Which put him in her mind—and her heart—over and over again.

The car turned right into a subdivision and wound through a rural neighborhood. Tucker held back, letting even more space grow between their cars. When they left the area and headed back to the road, Tucker said, "I think we've just been made."

Chapter Six

Elgin called Bengle again. "Hey, it's me. Where are you?"

"I'm leaving your place now. It's ready, but I have to tell you, you're asking for trouble."

"It'll be my trouble. She always was."

"Just leave me out of it. I've got enough of my own. Stupid Frost and his glorious ideas about getting laid." He grunted. "I sniffed around for the tremor all day. My feet are killing me. Torus isn't going to let us rest until we find at least one of our bastards. And it better be the one who killed that guy, because if it happens again, we're fried."

"Get in your car and meet me at the end of Foothills Road. I'm almost home, but I'm being tailed. I think it's Nikkita's daughter. She and the guy she's with might have picked me up at the apartment building. I could use some backup. It's been awhile since I've fought."

"She's not your daughter, right?"

Elgin's mouth turned into a snarl. "No." He could still see the man Nikkita had been shacking up with trying to protect her. That was *his* role, as her husband—not the job of some weak human who knew some karate moves. She'd never told the guy, obviously, that her husband was no match for any mere human defense. "They're looking for trouble, following me. They can both go."

"Be right there."

It had been a long time. Darkness shimmered over his hands as they tightened on the wheel. Those who held it were ordered to keep it under control. They were only to use it for their work.

The shimmer formed into two black paws, big as bears'. He felt the rush, the hunger for a fight, to free the dark energy that lay coiled inside him. Foothills Road was desolate, the east end of a defunct housing development not far from their base. He would make sure to leave nothing behind.

neighborhood's all but abandoned. If he's got her in the car, he may be planning to kill her here."

Del sucked in a breath at those words. That's probably what Elgin would do. Carrie was a loose end, just as Del and Tucker were. Trouble for Elgin.

"I'm going to turn around," Tucker said. "If he stays here, we'll be able to find him, but I got a bad feeling about following him any farther in."

He turned into a driveway and began to back out. Suddenly, another car came out of nowhere and blocked them.

"Hell." Tucker turned to the left and drove through the dirt yard. He'd nearly reached the road when Elgin's car pulled up in front of them. "He made us, all right. And he's got a friend." A shadow of fear flickered across his face, but that was the only thing that gave away what he was feeling. He reached over and squeezed her hand. "I'm going to leave the car running. Remember the plan. I'll distract them; you get to Elgin's car and see if your mother's there."

"I'm not going to leave you."

He was taking in the two men who were approaching their car. "No time to get sentimental. Can you remember an address?"

"Right now I can hardly breathe or think or anything."

He gave it to her anyway. "That's where I live. I'll meet you there. If I don't, tell the others what happened. Get in the driver's seat."

Her stomach cramped as Tucker stepped out of the car and closed the door. She hit the locks and climbed

Chapter Seven

Del gripped the edges of her seat. "What do we do now?"

"He's going to lead us somewhere where he can kill us. That's if he thinks or knows what we are. We could be a couple of punks out to rob him. Either way, he'll know what we are when we get close enough. And probably who we are."

So he wasn't backing down. That relieved her. And scared her.

"We're going to take him on, then?"

"It's the only chance we'll have to save your mother, if she's in the car."

"He's the one who tore apart my father. Tucker, I don't want you hurt."

"I can take care of myself. It's you I'm concerned about. You can't exactly psychometry him to death, now, can you?" He narrowed his eyes, scanning the area. "This into the driver's seat. The second man remained at the front of the car, his body tensed and ready. She saw the moment Elgin picked up the tremor, as Tucker called it. And the moment he recognized his own gray eyes looking back at him.

The man was definitely Tucker's father, though Elgin wasn't as wiry or muscular. He had the same subtle ways of registering emotion. Tucker stepped away from the car, leading Elgin, who mirrored his moves.

"You wanted to talk to me," Elgin said to Tucker.

This was going to start out civilly, but it wouldn't end that way. She saw again the flashes of violence and blood—the black beast tearing at her father—that she'd picked up from the ring.

Her fingers tightened on the wheel. *He killed my father. Killed him for no other reason than he was with my mother.* Now he had her, too. And Tucker.

"No. No!" She put the car into gear and lurched forward, aiming for Elgin. Obviously surprised, he didn't move fast enough to avoid the front corner of the car. It knocked him right into Tucker, throwing both men to the ground. The other guy grabbed for the passenger door but she jammed on the gas and dove to Elgin's green car.

He'd left his car running. She put the car into park and spilled out, stumbling as she reached for the door handle. Out of the corner of her eye, she saw a black beast loping toward her. She jumped into the Buick as a smoky paw reached for her. Felt its coldness as a claw sliced across her wrist. She yanked the door closed, trapping the paw. The beast yowled, and then the paw disappeared.

She jabbed the lock button and met the face of the beast on the other side of the window. He looked like a misshapen tiger, fangs unnaturally long. He smashed his paw against the glass; thank God it held.

"Mom," she called, having to push the word out of her throat.

"Del? No, please tell me he didn't get you." Her mother's voice, muffled in the trunk.

"We came to get you, Mom. Me and Tucker." She pulled away as the beast smashed at the window again, this time cracking it. "I'm getting you out of here."

Tucker! She frantically searched for him. He was racing across the dirt yard toward the moving car, Elgin right behind him.

Something landed on the roof, and a second later she heard the sound of an object hitting the windshield. She spun to see the glass crackled in a large spiral, the dark thing coming at it again. She turned back to Tucker in time to see him leap toward the car. As he left the ground, he morphed from man to a black blur, and then she heard him land on the roof with a heavy *thud*.

Elgin was right behind him, turning into a beast too as he jumped at the car. When he landed, there was a scuffle right above her.

"Oh, God, what have I done?"

The paw smashed through the windshield and grabbed her around the throat. She struggled to hold onto the wheel as it pulled her forward. He was going to pull her right through it and out. She clawed and pounded at the paw. It *felt* like an animal, hard and sinewy, but cold and smooth.

Suddenly its hold on her loosened, and two beasts rolled onto the hood. Tucker. One had to be Tucker. She rammed on the brakes when they both began tumbling off the front of the car. She couldn't risk running him over,.

A third beast reeled off the side of the roof when the car lurched to a stop. She couldn't tear her eyes from the two beasts fighting in front of her: the misshapen tiger and a wolf nearly as big. They looked like they were made of black quicksilver.

Tucker's that wolf.

Another paw smashed through the side window, tearing her attention from Tucker. All she could see in that panicked moment was a creature neither wolf nor panther, but eerily in between. Elgin. Even in Darkness, he had the gray eyes. A stream of rope-like smoke trailed into the car, to the ignition, and the engine died.

She missed the stream that unlocked the door. He jerked it open and morphed to man as he clamped his hand over her wrist before she could pull away. "Bengle, I'm taking off," he called to where the two beasts fought. "Finish him."

She couldn't free herself. "That's your son. You can't—"

He smacked her hard, sending her banging against the passenger door. Before the ringing in her ears stopped and the black spots cleared, he'd locked the doors and settled into the driver's seat.

"My son who would use the Darkness I gave him to kill me," he muttered.

She tried to get up from where she'd slid to the floor. He opened the glove box and pulled out a piece of rope, grabbing at her hands and tying her wrists. She fought him, and he gripped her arms so hard she expected to hear the snap of her bones. Then he shoved her back to the floor. Something hit the car on her side, then another *whump!* Tucker.

Elgin put the car into drive and lurched away. She tried to loosen her hands, but he'd cinched them tight. She stared at the lock switch. Could she move it?

Talk to him, cover the sound.

She focused on moving that lever. "What are you going to do with my mom?"

"Don't you want to know what I'm going to do to *you*? You should have been my daughter. Nikkita should have stayed. I didn't hunt her down before, but now . . . now everything's changed."

Because of the attack. She could hardly think about that—the locks clicked. He didn't seem to notice. She focused on the door pull now.

"Why? Mom didn't kill that man last night. Neither did your son."

She tightened the muscles in her legs, readying herself. The door opened and she threw herself against it, falling out and rolling. Not asphalt, her first thought. She landed hard, but on the packed dirt of what used to be someone's front yard.

As soon as she came to a stop, she heard a car engine. The world hadn't stopped spinning, and all she could see was the front of a car coming at her. She couldn't move fast enough to get out of the way. She cringed, ready for the impact.

"You all right?" Tucker's voice. He'd pulled up beside her, opened his door, and was helping her up.

She nodded as he hauled her into the car, got back in, and tore out. "He has my mom! She's in the trunk." She scrambled to a sitting position, looking for the green Buick. "Where is he?"

Tucker searched as he drove. "He used the Disappearing act. The one I inherited from him. I don't see him or his car anywhere. That's how they snuck up on us."

"We have to find her." The words ripped out of her.

He did a U-turn and went back to where they'd had the initial scuffle.

"Where's Bengle, the other one?" she asked.

"I hurt him pretty bad. When I saw Elgin get in the car with you—saw him *hit you*—I went nuts on him. He was trying to hold me down, to keep me from getting to you." He scanned the area. "I don't see him either."

She'd seen his expression go fierce when he'd said 'hit you.' It made her shiver. His hands were trembling as he shifted. She felt a frenetic energy vibrating from him. His hair was mussed, and he had several cuts and scrapes.

She held her bound wrists at him. "Can you cut me free?"

He blinked. "He tied you up that fast?"

"He had rope in the glove box." She swallowed hard. "Maybe left over from what he used on my mother. She was right there, in the trunk. I almost had her."

"The fastest way to cut the rope is to use my claw." He was warning her, giving her time to look away.

"Do it."

She neither watched nor turned, seeing a black paw in her peripheral vision. With a deft flick of his wrist, he cut the rope without ever touching her. The rope fell away. He pulled her hand toward him, his eyes narrowing as he took in the bloody scratch. His fingers tightened on her.

"Bastard," he spat.

She stared at the cut, too, remembering how visceral the beast looked, how real it felt. "You're a wolf." The word came out a whisper. It seemed a bizarre statement now, because he was entirely human.

He let go of her hand and continued driving, watching. "You choose the kind of creature you want to Become when you start working with Darkness. Otherwise you end up like that Bengle guy, sort of a hybrid. But you can use it in other ways."

"Like you did during your act. And Elgin, he used it that way, too. He turned off the car with a stream of it." She tried not to sound afraid. The effort strained her voice, giving it a sense of falseness. "We have to find her. Or I have to find her."

"What, you don't want my help now that you saw me Become?"

"No, it's not that. Tucker, you don't owe me risking your life to find her."

"It's way beyond that now, Del. These guys are after me, and the D'Rats."

"The D'Rats?"

"Desert Rats. They're my sort of family. I'm going to take those two out before they take us out."

He said it so casually, so coldly, she again remembered his words about not knowing him at all.

"How did it feel to see him? To finally face him?"

"It was strange, looking into my own eyes. But I felt nothing more than that. I'm a loose end, a problem. That's nothing new, but I sure as hell am not going to let him wipe me out because of it."

She was shaking now, feeling cold even though heat came out of the vents. Tucker was back on the highway, heading south. She saw him again, in her mind, Becoming wolf as he soared through the air. Graceful. Fast. Terrifying. He fought like a vicious animal. Even as he'd held her hand and looked at her scratch, she'd felt his anger over it.

"You're afraid of me now," he said, and she realized he'd been watching her ruminations.

She let out a long breath. "I've always been afraid of you, Tucker."

When he was a child, she was afraid they'd do something that would make him run away. Later, she was afraid to give into the longings of her developing body, afraid to love a boy who might not be able to love her back. Afraid of how he'd insinuated himself into the cells of her body, scared she'd never get him out. And after he'd gone, scared he was dead or in prison or even that he'd moved on and forgotten all about her.

He regarded her but didn't push her to reveal any of the reasons. "That's probably a good thing," he said at last. "Because we're going to be stuck together until we get rid of these two."

"Stuck?" That word shot comfort and something she didn't want to explore into her.

"I'm taking you to my place. You're staying there until we figure out what to do next."

Chapter Eight

FORTY MINUTES LATER, Del and Tucker pulled onto a street that seemed to be at the southern edge of nowhere in Hendersonville. She'd never ventured this far south in the Las Vegas Valley. There were a couple of short, paved streets off the main road, each with one or two homes on it. All around them were miles of scrubland and low mountains in the distance.

He swung the car into the driveway of a two-story hacienda-style home that looked well kept—pretty, even. There were four cars parked in the driveway. The sun had set, leaving a color-splashed sky to fade into night. Del tried to find comfort in that very ordinary sight as she stepped out. As if she didn't have enough to deal with, she was about to meet Tucker's comrades. She was afraid to ask how much they knew about her.

"It's nice," she said, walking beside him up the flagstone path to the front porch. The yard, like many in the area, was a sea of rocks interspersed with sculptured planting beds. "I like it."

"I found it a few months after I left your place. It was abandoned then, and the other house wasn't there yet, so no one noticed or cared that I was living here. I wasn't running drugs or anything." His voice lowered as they reached the front porch. "Just becoming a monster in the shadows." He glanced at her, maybe to see her reaction to that.

She kept her expression neutral as she took in the place. "So this is where you went." No air conditioning, no soft bed, but he'd had a roof over his head. She looked out over the miles of vacant land. "I can see why you chose the area. Lots of room to . . . run. I'm assuming you now live here legally."

"Bought it as soon as I could muster up a down payment."

He had a home. When he opened the door and gestured for her to walk in, she saw that he had a family, too. Three men—one in a wheelchair—and one woman sat in the living room, breaking out of what looked like a tense conversation.

The woman, close to Del's age, launched to her feet and threw herself into Tucker's arms. "You're okay." She squeezed her eyes shut, as though absorbing him. Then she leaned back and took him in, brushing her fingers over the scrapes on his cheek. They disappeared. Completely, magically disappeared. Del stared, but no one else seemed to think it was miraculous or even out of the ordinary.

The woman's eyes were way too big for her small features, fringed in thick lashes, and she wore not a stitch of makeup. Her long, blond curls were clipped up in a ponytail, and her sweats hung on what appeared to be a small frame.

Del felt a twinge of . . . well, it couldn't be jealousy, but it was a damned uncomfortable feeling as the girl smoothed her hand over every scratch and healed it. "I was so worried when Greer told me about your call." Only then did she turn to notice Del standing there. Her expression changed, shuttering. "Who are you?"

"Did you . . . heal him?" Del asked instead of answering, because she couldn't get her mind around what she'd seen.

She shifted her gaze to Tucker, as though checking with him before answering.

He nodded. "This is Delaney. Her mom's the one who took me in for a while and told me what I am."

They seemed to know at least that much. Maybe he hadn't told them he'd been kicked out.

He squeezed the woman's shoulder affectionately. "This is Shea. She can heal, though she's not supposed to waste it on bumps and bruises." He gave her an admonishing look. "She psychically takes on the injury herself. Speaking of, Del, you were hurt, too."

She waved it off, her wrist stinging at the movement. "I'm fine. I'll wash up later, put some stuff on it."

"You're sure?"

"Absolutely."

He gestured to the guy in the wheelchair. "That's

Darius. Next to him is Greer. And that's Cody with his hand in the potato chip bag, which is where it usually is."

Cody, with his teen-idol looks, smirked at him before nodding to her.

"Is she one of us?" Greer asked, coming closer, his gray eyes an odd juxtaposition to his warm Native American coloring as she'd expected. Tucker's half-brother then.

"Yes, but she doesn't have Darkness."

How many of them had it? Del supposed she'd find out if she stayed around them long enough.

She took them all in. "Nice to meet you."

"You, too," Greer said, and then turned to Tucker. "So what's going on?"

Tucker sat on the edge of the coffee table and filled them in. Halfway through, he realized she was still standing there and gestured for her to sit. Del took one of the chairs, a soft swivel recliner, and twisted back and forth as she listened to his telling of the events of the afternoon. All the terror and fear gripped her again. Her mother, gone. She felt so damned helpless, and she heard the same frustration in Tucker's voice when he finished with how they had no way to find Elgin.

Shea's eyes grew even wider, if that was possible. "They're looking for us. All of us."

Tucker nodded, and she wrapped her arms around herself. Greer put his hand on her shoulder, and for a moment she leaned into him. Then she shrugged away, getting to her feet. "What do we do?"

Tucker said, "We watch our backs. They don't know about us—"

"They know about you now," Del said,. "Because you helped me, Elgin knows you exist."

Shea turned on her. "You put him in the line of fire?" She looked at Tucker. "Is that true?"

Del thought the little spitfire might tear her head off.

Tucker took Shea by the shoulders. "They have her mother. I couldn't not try to get her back." He looked at the rest of them. "But they don't know about you. We want to keep it that way."

Darius wheeled forward. "We're not going to hide and wonder when they're going to nab us. We have to get them first."

"We don't know where they are. There are two of them. One is my and Greer's father. The other guy is named Bengle." Tucker met each of their gazes. "He didn't look like any of you."

Del took them in: Darius with his tight, angry expression; Greer big and brawny; Cody, who looked like a teenager with his fresh face and long lashes . . . and Tucker, whom she'd seen take on one of those creeps without hesitation. She didn't want to believe that any of them could have mauled that guy last night. But they could have, and she needed to keep that in mind.

Tucker said, "Shea, you should—"

"I know what you're going to say, and no, I'm not moving back here. I love my place, which isn't littered with dirty socks and towels and junk food. I can take care of myself." She gave him a meaningful look. Maybe healing wasn't the only thing she could do.

"Not against these guys," Tucker said.

Greer flexed his big hands, ready for the fight. "How did you take on the guy you fought?"

Del had wondered that, too, and leaned forward to hear his answer better. In fact, he had all of their attention.

"I kept shredding his Darkness. I went ape-shit on him, just flipped out. I must have swiped a thousand times, and I kept seeing bits of him flake off. He would pull them back, and he was so busy doing that, he wasn't properly fighting me. He made these sounds, like it hurt. I think it wore him down, weakened him."

"How do you kill them when they're in Darkness?" Del asked.

"We don't know," Tucker said. "We're the only ones we've been around who have it. So far we haven't wanted to kill each other." He shot them a sheepish raise of his eyebrow. "Mostly."

"We spar each other," Greer said. "Out in the desert. Tucker fell off a cliff once, hit a few rocks on his way down. He was kind of our test subject."

"I stayed in Darkness as I fell. It hurt, tore into me, but I was able to heal myself." Tucker faced her, probably seeing the horror of the picture Greer had put in her mind. "We're just rearranging our energy when we Become. We pull from the deepest part of ourselves, from the Darkness we hold inside."

He held out his hand, palm up, and that black spiral she'd seen him make earlier appeared. It writhed up like a quicksilver snake. He flicked at it, making it tremble. "I can feel it when I do this. It's like this bit is part of me, part of my energy."

Darius reached over and swiped it, making it go *poof.* "If you break off a part of it, it takes time to regenerate it."

Tucker smacked him on the side of his head. "I can handle the demo."

Darius reared up in an instinctive response. Even though he was in a wheelchair, he looked every bit as dangerous as Tucker. Which made her wonder: could he walk while in Darkness?

Tucker met his gaze, daring him. A few tense moments passed. Darius's shoulders relaxed, and he turned away first.

Tucker held his ground for a few seconds longer, and then turned to Shea. He kept Darius in sight, though. "Shea, order a round of pizzas."

"Please," she said, with a tilt of her head.

He chucked her on the chin. "Please, doll."

The endearment prickled through Del, as much as the obvious affection Shea felt for him did.

When Shea turned to go into the kitchen, Greer said to her, "You'd lay me flat if I called you something like that."

Shea paused in the doorway, her fingers tightening on the frame. "It's different with Tuck."

Mm, there were some interesting dynamics going on here, ones Del wasn't entirely comfortable with. Not that she was comfortable with any of this, or these people. And that especially included Tucker.

Chapter Nine

"WHAT DID YOU do to my daughter?" Carrie had been screaming that ever since the car had lurched away twenty minutes ago. She'd heard car doors opening, closing . . . engines racing off . . . glass smashing. She was insane with worry. Now the car had stopped, and a garage door closed.

He opened the trunk, and the question scratched out of her hoarse throat again.

"I tried to bring her to the party, but she obviously inherited your skill for telekinesis. She escaped, helped by her boyfriend."

Carrie wilted in relief, barely fighting him when he carried her from the garage, through the kitchen, and to a back bedroom.

She knew there was no point in trying to escape. Not with him. If she cooperated, maybe he'd grant her one request: leave her daughter alone.

Carrie watched Elgin stalk around the bed where he tied her. It wasn't the same house they'd shared all those years ago. From what little she'd seen of it, it was tidy and neutral.

He sat on the edge of the bed, hovering over her. "Torus ordered me to kill you when you ran off. But I didn't."

"No, you killed the man I loved," she hissed.

He slapped her, the sting setting the side of her face on fire. "You are my wife. You belong with me, with our people. But you left us all, breaking the rules you promised to obey when you came here. It was my job to find you, and when I did, I saw you with *him*. Darkness took over. You brought on his death. You murdered him as much I did."

She closed her eyes and rolled her head to the side. Yes, she had.

He pinched her chin and forced her to look at him. "I let you live, Nikkita. Or is it Carrie now? Do you like that name better?" His voice was a taunt. "Did that separate you more from what you are? You pretty fool. When you ran that night, I let you go. I told Torus I'd killed you, stashed your body. If I'd known you were pregnant . . ."

The mention of Del shot fear into her. "Don't hurt her. She has nothing to do with this. *I* left you. I betrayed you; at least that's how you see it. So punish me, not her."

He sat back, as though considering her words. "Who was the man with her?"

Had she heard Del right? "I couldn't see who was with her. I was in the trunk, if you'll recall."

"Your daughter came to rescue you, brave little thing. She tried to run me down. You must be very proud."

She was, dammit—proud and scared for her reckless daughter.

"You know who she would ask for help." He leaned closer, his voice low and harsh. "He had my eyes. My looks. Come on, Nik. Don't tell me you have no idea who that kid was."

"He's your son; at least I figured he was. But you already know that."

He gripped her face again, leaning so close she could feel his breath on her chin. "But who is he to you? To your daughter?"

"He's just some punk. My daughter felt a draw to him, brought him home for dinner one night, years ago. When I sensed what he was, what he held, I sent him away. I didn't want him near her."

His mouth tightened into a hard line. "Because he's like me."

She nodded.

"A monster. That's what you called me the first time I Became in front of you. Interesting that your daughter brought home my son." He laughed. "That must have been deliciously ironic." His smile faded. "But you rejected us both. Seems like you can't get rid of Darkness. Because here I am. And there he was. Tell me everything you know about him: where he lives, what he does."

"They haven't seen each other in years, so if he's with her, I have no idea how or why. He was a kid the last time

I saw him. How should I know what he does or where he lives?" That much was true. "Leave them alone. They're no threat to you." She didn't want him to know that Tucker had lived with them. The less he knew of him, the better.

"But they are. Someone killed a man last night. Torus wants a clean sweep of any loose ends we might have left. My son is one. Your daughter is another."

"My daughter certainly didn't kill that man. Leave her alone."

"No, she didn't, but she holds our DNA. And your abilities, which could bring unwanted attention to her."

Carrie couldn't help the whimper that escaped her throat. She would beg, if she had to, but it wouldn't matter. There was no reasoning with Elgin. But he wasn't the cold man she remembered. Now she saw heat in his eyes. Anger.

He still held her face, but with less pressure. "The last time I found you, I watched you before I made my presence known. You never touched me like you did him. Never wanted me like that. No, you cowed away from me. Even before I tapped into Darkness, you didn't want me like that. Why him and not me?"

Was he actually hurt by her rejection?

"You had no emotions. No heart. No tenderness. You wanted me but you didn't love me."

"You complained that I was cold. You were the oddball, with your feelings and desires. When I heard that Darkness brought passion, I tapped into it for you."

She shook her head. "No. Don't say that."

He gave her a grave nod that sunk her stomach. How many ruined lives could she be responsible for? How many losses?

Now he stroked his fingers down the sides of her cheeks. "You were always mine. I feel you inside me. As angry as I am with you, I don't want to kill you. The problem is you're supposed to be dead. Others live nearby, and if they know you're here, they'll report it to Torus. He'll kill you, and me, too. I've lost enough because of you." He placed his hand over the front of his pants. "Do you want to know how Torus punished us for resorting to the company of human women? He castrated us, thinking that would kill our desire."

She sucked in a breath, and yet, felt a sense of relief. But no, she didn't see a lack of desire in his eyes. "I'm so sorry."

Beneath his hand, though, she saw a bulge form. Was he lying? He looked smug.

"I discovered a new way to use Darkness. It's amazing how it can be manipulated."

Horror froze her as she put it together. She tried to wipe it from her face, turning away.

He crawled into the bed with her, laying his leg on top of her, his arm across her chest. "I want to spend a little quality time with you. And if you beg enough, if you do everything I ask, maybe I'll consider your request to let your daughter live."

She turned to face him, trying to judge whether he was telling the truth. "What about Tucker?" As soon as his name was out of her mouth, she cringed.

"Is that his name? You'll have to do better than that. You'll have to give me his last name. In fact, you may be able to help me more than that." He leaned closer, his mouth grazing hers. "Because I'm willing to bet that you'll give me anything I ask for to save your daughter. Your body. Your cooperation. And even Tucker."

Chapter Ten

TUCKER LED DEL up the stairs. He stopped when they reached the top, turning and taking her hand. A strange quiver passed through her.

He turned it palm up. "That's more than nothing, Del. I should have asked Shea to—"

She shook her head. "No, that's all right. It's fine."

"You've got bruises on your wrists." Anger vibrated from him.

"I wasn't being very cooperative when he was trying to bind them." She gently pulled her hand away. "I'm fine. Really."

He led her into the last bedroom on the left. His, she guessed. Big furniture was crowded into the small space. Otherwise, it wasn't far from the way his room had looked when he'd lived with them: clothes draped over the back of a chair, Dean Koontz books here and there, and four decks of cards on top of the dresser. Several cards had spilled out of one box and landed on the wood floor. She saw pieces of paper and business cards with room numbers written in feminine handwriting.

She followed him to a large, luxurious bathroom. The granite counter had the kinds of porcelain sinks that sat on top like bowls. The large glass shower looked incredibly inviting.

He let go of her hand and rifled through a medicine cabinet, pulling out salve and antiseptic. Then he ran the water until it was warm and rubbed soap on a washcloth. He took her hand again. In the brighter lights, it looked much worse than it felt, the blood crusted over and the surrounding skin red.

He kept his concentration on that, but she couldn't take her eyes from him. His hair was still mussed, and she resisted the urge to comb her fingers through the thick, shiny strands. He was gentle, taking great care with her. Her heart tightened uncomfortably, making the tingle of pain on her arm nothing in comparison.

He's unnatural. Supernatural. She had to remind herself, crazily enough, since she'd just seen him turn into something resembling a wolf. But here, he was a man, his humanity in full control, tending to her wound.

He is a man. You know his heart, once felt his body pressed against yours.

She shook the thoughts away, catching his attention.

"Does it hurt?" he asked, catching her off guard with the tenderness in his eyes.

"A little." *A lot. But not the arm, Tucker. Not even*

close. "Thank you for helping me. For trying to rescue my mom."

"We're not giving up yet. When you give up, you die."

He spoke from experience. He turned back to his task, releasing her from the hold his silver eyes had on her. After rubbing on the salve, he clamped her hand between his arm and his side and wrapped some gauze around her wrist.

"There, you're all set," he said, releasing her.

Her cell phone rang. She dug in the purse she'd slung over her shoulder and stared at the screen. "I don't recognize the number."

He gestured for her to take it as he came up beside her and pressed his cheek to hers to listen.

"Hello," she answered.

"It's me. Mom. I want you to know that I'm okay. I wasn't supposed to leave my people, and I did. I broke the rules and it's time for me to go back to them, maybe back home. Elgin promised he wouldn't hurt you, but . . . only if he can talk to Tucker. Alone. He wants to meet his son. He says he won't hurt him and I believe . . . no, I don't—"

The line went dead.

Del called the number back, and this time a man answered. Elgin.

"I want to talk to my mother," she said.

"You heard, she's fine. She wants you to go on with your life, and I have promised that if she cooperates, I will let you live."

"What are you going to do to her?"

"She'll likely go home, where she can't get into trouble."

Home. Her mother had said her dimension was a lot like this one. Obviously, though, she was happier here.

"What do you want with Tucker?" Del asked.

"He's my son. I want to get to know him."

Tucker took control of the phone. "Where?"

Del now leaned close to him to hear. "Seems you could find Foothills Road again. Why don't we meet there tomorrow morning, at six? We got off to a rocky start, what with your girlfriend trying to run me down."

"She's not my girlfriend," he was quick to say. "I'm helping her, that's all."

Del strained to hear her mom in the background. Why had she been cut off? What had she been about to say?

"You can help her by meeting with me. I think we can come to an understanding."

"I'll be there." Tucker disconnected.

She gripped his arm. "You're not going to meet him. You heard him: they're rounding up the loose ends. He'll crucify you as the one who killed that man."

"I know he's not going to be there with his arms open wide." He muttered something, jamming his fingers back through his hair. "It gives me the chance to kill him. And you're staying out of it."

It hit her then. "Oh, my God. He's making a deal. Me for you. That's it, isn't it? He'll let me live if you . . . die."

"That's only if he can get me."

"But he'll have at least one other guy there. You'll be outnumbered."

"That's my problem. I'm not bringing in any of the D'Rats. I can't afford for those guys to know about them."

"They already know about me."

"No way, Del. You can't fight them."

"I can move things. That's how I got out of the car." She turned to his dresser and pushed her hand toward it. More of those cards slid to the floor. She did it again, and two business cards flew off. "Okay, it's not lethal, but it's a start." She knocked a bottle of cologne off but caught it before it hit the floor. A whiff of a citrus scent filled the air.

"You're not going with me." He picked up the cards and slapped them down on the dresser. "Your mom was saying what he told her to, trying to convince me she believed him. It's her only hope of saving you."

"No, she wouldn't do that."

"I understand. I'd do it, too. Just like I'd send some potentially dangerous kid away from my daughter."

"You *are* doing it. And she couldn't go through with it. That's why he disconnected the call. She couldn't do it, Tuck."

He nodded in acknowledgment. "I know what to expect. I'll be ready."

"So will he."

"I can handle myself. You're not coming. End of discussion. Come on, I'll show you to your room. You look exhausted."

The conversation wasn't over. Not by a long shot. Leave Tucker to the mercy of that dark bastard? No way.

"This was Shea's room," Tucker said. He pushed open the door. "There's not much here, a bed and dresser, but it'll do." He walked to the closet and slid the door open. "She left some clothes here, so you're welcome to wear them. She never did."

Given how the girl dressed, it was a surprise to see two pretty dresses hanging in there. "It's a shame. They're beautiful." She ran her fingers down the silky fabric, her fingers brushing the tag that was still on one of them.

"Greer gave them to her for Christmas, trying to help her find her feminine side, I guess. What you saw her in, that's what she wears: jeans, baggy shirts. Greer accidentally walked in on her as she was getting out of the shower. He was shocked at the curves she's hiding. It woke him up big time, but it's made things tense between them."

"She hides herself," Del said.

"Playing therapist?"

"I guess. Someone hurt her. Abused her, when she was young. She may blame her body, her curves, for bringing that kind of attention."

"I know she's had a tough childhood, but I don't know all the details."

"You . . . seem to have a special bond with her."

He met her gaze, trying to read what her real question was, maybe. "Yeah, we do. She's terrific, smart, strong."

"And you love her." She could see it in his eyes, his deep affection for Shea.

Her heart dropped when he nodded. "But if you're asking if I'm in love with her, no. It's not like that. I don't fall in love with every girl I live with."

Del pulled down a dress and held it up to her to hide the crazy relief she felt, and the more dangerous feeling his admission had curling through her: he'd fallen in love with her all those years ago. In love, not hormonal lust. "She's way smaller than I am."

He reached up to the top shelf in the closet and pulled out a blanket. Del took it from him, and then he reached farther back and pulled out some sweats. "I guess she left some of these, too. They'll do until we can get you some clothes."

"Thanks. I could use a shower."

"Sure." He nodded for her to follow to the hall.

How much did he carry on those broad shoulders? The well-being of his family. Now, the burden of her. Tomorrow morning, he would meet his father, and it wasn't going to be pretty.

He opened a door and pulled it shut again with a shake of his head. "You don't want to go in there. Greer and Cody share that one. Use mine."

Several minutes later, she was standing in the glass shower with hot water pounding against her back. God, her body hurt, her heart hurt, and her head felt as though it was going to explode with everything inside it. In the midst of all that, she placed her hands on the glass for balance and got a flash of an image: a woman's hands flattened against the glass, a man's hands over hers, his fingers entwined with hers. And the feeling of . . . sexual arousal. She jerked back, blinking at the surprise of it, more so at the way it heated her body.

Of course, Tucker brought women here, showered with them, made love to them.

Shaken, she continued washing her body, running the washcloth over her breasts, down her stomach. Her gaze kept going back to that spot on the glass. Now was not the time to get caught up in that. But oh, she did need to put her thoughts elsewhere. Those images pulled at a body so hungry for touch, for sexual intimacy, her mind swam with it.

"No. Stop it."

On top of everything else wrong about indulging her desire, it was spying, a personal invasion of Tucker's privacy.

She ran the washcloth up her legs, into the intimate places that felt alive, vibrating. She rinsed the cloth and hung it up, started to turn off the shower. Her gaze went right to the spot again.

Okay, one more time, just for a second. To escape, to . . . feel something I haven't felt in years.

Since Tucker.

Not only his hands on her, not only the promise of much more, but the way he made her feel inside. She'd never felt that with any other guy, even the ones she'd slept with.

Because you compare every man you meet to Tucker.

Damn, her mom was right.

She placed her hands on the spot, and the vision knocked her head back, coming at her in full color, full feeling, full everything. She was in the same position that the woman had probably been in when Tucker had come up behind her.

She felt the woman's feelings, sensations, since her hands had touched the glass. It was Del who felt him sliding in, filling her, the rise of the orgasm, pressure building, his hands now on her wet body, sliding over her breasts, pulling her closer, deeper—

"Del, you okay in there?"

Her eyes snapped open as she stumbled back, nearly loosing her footing on the tile floor. Had she groaned out loud? "I'm fine," she said, flipping off the water lever and grabbing for a towel. Her cheeks stung with embarrassment. "Just achy."

She took her time drying off, blow-drying her hair, looking at her blurry reflection in the steamy mirror.

She put more salve on her cut and rewrapped the gauze she'd removed before getting in the shower. She hoped he wouldn't mind that she put on his robe. Once it was tied around her, she breathed him in, the scent of soap and clean male. She had to go right to her room, no stopping, no talking. Maybe he wouldn't be in his room. That would be better.

Except he was, sitting on the bed straightening the wrinkled bills from the wooden box. His hair was damp, and he wore only jeans, obviously having taken a shower in the dirty bathroom. He looked up at her, and she had to remember to put some expression on her face that wouldn't give away her turmoil.

"Profitable day?" Despite her intentions, she found

herself sinking onto the corner of the bed, her hand on the big wooden ball at the corner of the footboard.

He shrugged. "Good as any." He paused, looking at the wad in his hand, now in a neat stack. Was he remembering when she'd thrown the bills up in the air? "Money used to mean everything to me. Now it's just pieces of paper compared to what's really important."

"And what's that?"

He stared hard at those bills. "The people I care about."

She didn't know if he included her in that statement, wasn't going to ask. She doubted it. "Do you like doing street shows?"

"Yeah. I'm my own boss, set my own hours. I get some punk trying to encroach in my territory every now and then, but they come to a quick understanding once we have a little chat."

"Mm, I bet." She remembered those cold eyes, his dangerous energy. "You're good at it. A natural entertainer."

His fingers moved in an automatic way, finishing the pile. "There's a particular satisfaction you get when you make people happy, when you can surprise them." He surprised her by handing her the stack. "You won't be able to go home until Elgin is dead. You'll stay here until then. This is for clothes and whatever else you need."

What she needed couldn't be bought: her mother home safe.

Tucker.

She blinked at the thought. She took the stack, their fingers brushing. "Why are you doing all this? You could have—should have—told me to get lost."

He got up from the bed and set the box on the end of the long dresser. "I couldn't turn you away, much as I wanted to. I meant what I said earlier; you gave me a safe, stable home for the first time, made me feel worthwhile. I decided to help you because I owe you and her for that. I own my home outright, pay taxes, am a generally upstanding citizen. That's because of you."

She stood, intending to go to her room, but her body wouldn't go past him. "You don't owe us." She gestured to his room, the house in general. "You've done well with your life, which you would have done even if you hadn't come into our lives. That's who you are. I'm proud of you. Of who you've become." She wanted to touch him, her fingers flexing with her need.

Apparently he sensed it. "It's not smart, you being in my bedroom with me."

"I know. I can't seem to make myself leave."

She put her hand on his chest, her palm pressing against his skin. He flattened his hand over hers, and in that moment she could see every hurt he'd suffered shadow his eyes. Then they shuttered, and he curled his fingers over hers and pulled her hand away.

"Don't touch me, Del. Don't ask if I love someone else with that look on your face that makes me think you're scared I'm going to say yes. Don't look at me like you want to save my soul."

"Your soul doesn't need saving. All I want to do is try to take away some of the pain my mom and I caused." She ran her hands over his hair, his face. "Would it help to know how my heart was torn out, too? How I cried every night for weeks, worried about you, looked for you. How I tried to make it better with every child I helped. How I never found anyone who made me feel like I did with you."

She pulled his hand to her mouth, kissing the back of it, the ridges of his veins, his knuckles, watching him crumble bit by bit. His eyes closed, and he tilted his head back. Then he pulled her into his arms, and she heard an agonized groan come from somewhere in his chest.

Her cheek came to rest against his chest and her hands went around his strong back. She could breathe for the first time in what felt like hours, since those texts. He held her stiffly, as though he didn't trust himself to relax into it.

She leaned closer against him. His arms went around her and pulled her closer. His jaw rested on her head, and his fingers flexed against her shoulders enough that she could feel it through the robe.

"Go," he said, his voice throaty, hoarse against the top of her head. But he made no move to release her.

"You're afraid you'll fall into some dark abyss, that you'll fall to your Darkness."

She felt him nod.

He said, "You saw what I am. If I let myself go there, I will feel like you are mine. You're already in me."

She stepped back, looking at him. He was beautiful, even in his pain, because she saw his longing, recognized it because it burned in her. "I'm leaving." But she didn't move away either.

Instead, she leaned forward and touched her mouth

to his. He kissed her, tenderly, his thumbs rubbing at her jawline, down the sides of her throat. She was sixteen again, sinking into that innocent, yet not-so-innocent time in the living room, kissing in a rainfall of money. Her hands slid down his back, absorbing the feel of him, wishing she could sink right into him.

She untied the belt of her robe, letting it slide over her shoulders and fall to the floor. The cool air stippled her skin, but the heat of his gaze warmed her from the inside.

He cherished her with his eyes, taking her in, tracing his fingers down her collarbone, down the inside of the curve of her breast, and down her stomach. "Del," he whispered, kissing her again, more fervently now. He ran his hands down her backside, cupping her ass and squeezing her to pull her harder against him.

Even through the jeans, she could feel the hard ridge of him. "Let me love you, Tuck," she murmured between kisses.

He unzipped his jeans and shoved them to the floor. She closed her eyes at the feel of his naked body against hers. In that brief glimpse of him, he looked beautiful, his muscles gilded in the light, his face in shadow. That body *felt* beautiful, hard, and warm, with the brush of the hairs of his legs against hers.

He eased her down on the bed, his thigh between hers, covering her with his body. His hands pinned hers on the mattress, his mouth kissing hers, his knee rubbing up and down her inner thigh. He caressed her breasts, trailing his thumb around her nipples, giving every bit of his concentration to what he was doing. He skimmed across her stomach, cupping her pubic area, and then feathering her inner thighs. She reached up to run her fingers through his hair, so soft and silky, black as night. He slid his finger into her folds, drawing a breath from her, stealing it away as he continued to stroke.

No, she wasn't smart to be here in his room, in his bed, but she could be nowhere else. She slipped her hand around the back of his neck and buried her face there as her body shuddered. Soft, breathy sounds came from deep in her chest as she wrapped her body around his. He didn't rush to move on to his pleasure. He kept pleasuring her, touching her, as though he couldn't get enough of her, rubbing up and down her back, the curve of her ass and down into the damp crevices he'd just driven her crazy touching.

She wrapped her fingers around his shaft, moving against him. He moved in sync with her, his hands at her hips. Her thumb slid over the tip of him, down the ridge of skin that made him suck in a breath and tighten his grip on her.

Now, she thought, and he must have read her mind, because he leaned over to the drawer in the nightstand and pulled out a condom. He ripped open the package and slid the sheath down the length of him. He, of all people, would never be reckless with sex.

She hooked her hands around the back of his neck and rolled onto her back, wanting the position that offered the most contact. He braced himself while she guided him in. He filled her, and it was in that, in his arms on either side sheltering her, that she realized how much her soul had craved him.

He watched her face as he entered her, and whatever he saw there gave him the go-ahead to move. She gripped his shoulders, squeezing, urging him deeper by wrapping her legs around his hips. He kissed her as he moved, softly murmuring her name, taking his time. After several minutes, Tucker rolled them over so she was on top.

Her brown hair became a curtain as she leaned down and nibbled at his jaw, his ear, and then his neck, keeping that slow, delicious rhythm. He caressed her breasts, making her roll her head back in pleasure, and then slid his hands down to her waist. As she rocked back and forth, he touched her already sensitive nub, using her own movements to send her over the edge again. When she went, she felt him shudder and throb inside her, his hands squeezing her hips hard. His eyes rolled back, head tilted as his orgasm shuddered through him.

She watched him slowly come back to himself, his jaw relaxing, his eyes opening to find her gaze on him. She couldn't help her smile, soft from her own exhaustion and satisfaction.

He had said her name, not the names of any of those other women he'd been with—their numbers on those pieces of paper and business cards—or that woman in the shower.

His chest rose and fell with his breaths; his face was flushed. He entwined his fingers with hers, pulling her close to kiss her. His tongue toyed with hers, sliding along the edge of her teeth. He finished the kiss, and then pulled her down so that her cheek rested on his chest, his arm over her shoulders to hold her close.

She flattened her hand on his stomach, his heartbeat thudding in her ear. She could feel him. Not just physically, but deep inside her. They remained for several long minutes. She felt his body tightening rather than becoming more relaxed and lifted her cheek from his chest.

He put his hand over his eyes. "Now we've gone and done it."

"Tucker . . . I'm not sorry this happened. I hope you aren't."

He sat up on his elbows. "Are you sure? Nothing's changed. I still hold Darkness."

"I'm okay with that."

"Are you?" He turned to black mist, then transformed to wolf. She involuntarily shrank back—exactly what he'd intended, she realized. "You'll always be afraid of me, Del."

The images of her father's death tangled in her mind with those animals she'd seen fighting on top of the car.

He's not the man who attacked your father.

But he comes from that man.

As her thoughts warred, he jumped to the floor, his movements as graceful as the real animal, four feet landing without a sound. But he was nothing like the real thing, his texture smooth, his essence like black liquid. He took several steps away and then morphed back to man, beautifully naked.

He rubbed the ball at the corner of the headboard and looked at her, as though he was warring with his own thoughts. "There's a part of you that will always be afraid of me. And there's a part of me that will die every time I see your fear. Get some sleep." He grabbed his discarded clothes and walked out.

Sleep? Was he frickin' kidding after breaking her heart with those words?

She got up and pulled on her robe. *I shouldn't do this. I really shouldn't.*

Her hands covered that ball, and she closed her eyes at the impact of his emotions. Not as strong because of the wood, but discernible. Pain. Yes, she'd hurt him again by turning away. By being afraid. But hey, he was an animal that wasn't an animal that was . . . whatever the hell Darkness was. He'd pushed her, Becoming like that, testing her, and now he was sure she would never accept that part of him.

Maybe she couldn't, not with what she'd seen from her father's ring. So she would walk away from him and be done with it once this was over.

She settled with that thought, but it didn't settle with her. No, she couldn't do that. Because he was inside her, too. *Fine mess you've gotten yourself into.*

She held on and went back to the moments before. He'd morphed from man to smoke to wolf in one instant of grace. The animal was terrifying, but it was beautiful, too, in its lines of muscle and liquid steel. He was perfectly formed, the snout long, his eyes shimmering.

Tucker's eyes. *Inside, he's still the man you love.*

That's what she felt most of all, holding onto the link between them. She could feel Tucker in his Darkness. She'd been right; he did have a good heart.

She went out to the hallway and heard the front door

close. He'd gone outside. She went downstairs, opened the door and peered out. No sign of him. Of course, he'd blend into the dark now. Fine, she'd go back to his bed and wait. It would give her time to sort through what she wanted to say to him. To see if what they had could be salvaged.

Chapter Eleven

TUCKER RETURNED FROM his run exhausted and trembling. His bedroom light was still on. Willing himself to smoke, he crept up the side of the house and looked in the window. Del was asleep on his bed, lying crossways. He watched her, with the moonlight washing over her face. God, she was beautiful.

What the hell did you do, Tuck?

He understood what he'd done, because he could feel it in the way he breathed her in and knew he would do anything for her. He'd crossed the line with her, with himself. Which is why he'd Become, without easing her in or warning her. He'd done what he could to push her away.

He drifted down and morphed to man. It was four in the morning. He was not going to let her go with him, and he knew she would fight him on it. Blue lights played on the stairs as he walked inside the house. Greer had fallen asleep on the couch again.

Tucker looked for his boots near the front door, where they all piled their shoes.

"Where are you going?"

Greer wasn't asleep after all. Tucker told him about the phone call.

Greer launched off the sofa. "That son of a bitch could be my father, too."

"You're not coming. They don't know about you." Which reminded him. He set his wallet on the end table. If something happened, he didn't want Elgin to find his home. Their home. That was probably how he'd gotten to Carrie's place. "I'm going early to recon the area. I'll be waiting when he gets there. I'm betting the second guy will get there early too and find a hiding spot. I'll take him out before Elgin even knows I'm there. Then it'll be him and me. I can take him."

"I'm going with you, Tucker."

Tucker shook his head. "Someone's got to watch over the D'Rats if something happens to me. Darius is too . . . well, Darius. Cody isn't the paternal type. Shea's strong, but the guys won't let her boss them around. But they need someone to guide them." He glanced back at the stairs. "And Del. Take care of her, too."

Greer's eyes narrowed. "You've got it for her, don't you?"

He was going to deny it but nodded instead. "I've had it for her for a long time. But she was out of my life and I told myself if I ever saw her, it wouldn't matter. It worked, at least the first time. Then she came back . . . and needed me."

"That'll get you every time." Tucker knew he was thinking of Shea by the shadow in his eyes. Especially since she'd been having trouble with a creepy "secret admirer." He seemed to study Tucker. "Scary shit, isn't it?" He ran his hand back over his hair. "It can make you crazy."

"Yeah." Part of the reason Shea had moved out was because of the tension between Darius and Greer, who both felt an attraction to her. He suspected it not only made her uncomfortable, but scared her that the two might fight because of her. She felt responsible, because she was attracted to both of them. As Del had surmised, Shea wouldn't let herself experience those kinds of feelings. That didn't mean that the two men didn't pick up on them, though.

Tucker glanced back at the stairs. "But as soon as this is over, it's over between Del and me, too. Our father killed hers in a jealous frenzy. She'll always look at me and see the beast that I am. I can't blame her for that." It hurt, yes, but he understood. "I hope to be back before she wakes, so I can tell her it's over. Hopefully I'll have her mother. Promise me you will stay put. Promise, Greer."

They took promises seriously, because no one had ever been reliable in their lives.

"All right, I promise, as long as you promise to call me if you need help."

"I will."

"Take Darius."

"Take me where?" Darius wheeled into the living room.

How long had he been lurking in the hallway? The guy sometimes made Tucker uneasy. He could see Greer stiffen.

"I'm going to face off with my biological father, and probably his buddy. I'm leaving Greer here, in charge."

Darius's eyes darkened as he gave Greer a lift of his chin. "Not in charge of me." He turned back to Tucker. "I'm in. Let me get dressed."

"I don't know if that's the best idea," Tucker said under his breath once the door had slammed shut.

"If he's going to go nuts on someone, let it be one of those bastards."

Tucker had been the only thing between the two of them once, when their feelings for Shea hit a flashpoint. Luckily, they both saw Tucker's relationship with her for what it is, more brotherly than anything else.

Darius burst out of his bedroom, wheeling up to them. "Let's go kick some ass."

Tucker laid out the map and went over the neighborhood and the plan. Then they looked at the satellite view on the Internet. "Got it?"

Darius nodded. "I am so ready to take these guys out."

Too ready. It's not like he could warn Darius not to go crazy on these guys, after what Tucker had done to Bengle. He met Greer's eyes. "If Del wakes up, keep her here. She knows where we're meeting, but she doesn't have a car." He gave him a chagrinned smile. "You'll have your own battle, I imagine. She's not going to be happy to be left behind."

"I know the feeling, but I can handle her. You." He gave Tucker a hug, patting his back. "Be careful." He didn't say the same to Darius, only gave him a nod that was supposed to convey the sentiment, Tucker imagined.

Darius drove his car, which was fitted to be driven completely with his hands. He was on edge during the drive, his entire upper body in constant motion. Fingers tapped his thighs, and every five minutes he looked in the rearview mirror to see if anyone was following. His wheelchair was in the back. The guy got around amazingly well in it, maneuvering into the car with ease.

"I don't like the closed loop," Darius said as they neared the area. "With the recent rain, the ground's going to be soft. From what you described, they trapped you last time."

"We won't be running because they'll be dead."

"Yeah, I like the sound of that. Ever killed someone, Tuck?"

The question took him off guard. "Yeah. Once. You?"

"Stabbed a guy who was trying to rob me. I came out of a bar, knew he was stalking me. So I acted drunk, singing and shit. He figured, guy in a chair, easy take." Darius smiled. "He got a little surprise."

"You have to be careful, dude. Using Darkness is a last-resort option, especially in public."

Darius flicked a glance his way. "Is that why you're the Alpha, 'cause you're the sensible one?"

Tucker laughed, despite Darius's adversarial tone. "There is no Alpha. We're not a wolf pack."

"But we are a pack, and you are in charge."

"I'm in charge because I'm the one who found all of you. I own the house most of you live in. But sensible? Not always."

"I'm looking for my own place. Nothing personal, but I need space, privacy."

"Yeah, there's not a lot of that." He wouldn't mind if Darius moved out. The tension between him and Greer was annoying at times. "Okay, let me out here. At six, start down Foothills Road, nice and slow." Darius was supposed to sit there for a few minutes, drawing out Elgin. Hopefully by then, this Bengle guy would be out of the picture. "If Elgin approaches the car, I'll be behind him. Your windows are dark enough that he won't see it's not me in the car. Don't do anything stupid."

Darius lifted his upper lip in a snarl. "And try not to get yourself killed. I'd hate to have to console your girlfriend."

Tucker had to stop himself from slamming the door closed. Darius liked to rile people, and Tucker wasn't about to let him. He closed the door softly, even though they were a distance from Foothills.

Darkness transformed everything, including his clothing. He let it claim him, becoming the smoke that had scared the hell out of him the first few times he'd Become. Becoming *nothing* for a few moments before forming into the denser energy of Darkness still stepped up his heartbeat. He'd chosen wolf for his form, drawn to them since he was a kid. Now, sometimes, when he roamed the desert in Darkness, he'd see one. Of course, the animals would take off the moment they sensed something supernatural in their midst.

He felt the dirt beneath his paws, the cold air, and the colder coat of not fur but energy. Gaining his sense of direction, he tore off into the direction of the Foothills.

ELGIN GOT UP and dressed. "If only you'd cooperated like that before, we wouldn't be in this predicament."

She had merely tolerated him, but at least he'd had the pleasure of penetration, of touching her, if not ejaculation. That was a pleasure he would never have again because of her. More so, he had the pleasure of forcing her to do as he wanted.

"I never meant for you to tap into some kind of black magic to satisfy me," she said, her voice without inflection. "Our marriage wasn't about love or attraction. You needed a wife, I needed a husband. That's all it was."

"But you had certain obligations as my wife. You took your pleasure elsewhere."

"I didn't mean to fall in love." Her mouth stretched into a frown, probably remembering the weak human.

"That was the price you paid for straying. We all pay a price for our sins, Nikkita."

"I've paid, Elgin. Please keep your word. Don't hurt my daughter. Or Tucker."

"I never said anything about Tucker. And why do you care about him? You said he was a punk kid you sent . . . ah, you fell for him, too, didn't you? Maybe not romantically, but you've got a soft spot in your heart for him. Sorry, dear, but I can't let him live. He doesn't only carry my genes; he carries something that could expose us. And if he's the one who killed that guy, and he goes on to kill someone else, it's my head on the chopping block. Again. I'll bet my boy doesn't know he may have another capability; he may not have inherited it at all."

He held out his hand to her, focusing the power of his energy at her. It hit her like a wave, throwing her head back, a painful grimace as she writhed and grunted as though seizing. He held her there for a few seconds, enjoying making her suffer as he had suffered all these years. When he dropped his hand, she collapsed with a groan.

The Force was painful for others. It had another effect for those with Darkness. As Tucker would soon find out.

Chapter Twelve

DEL WOKE WITH a start, immediately aware that Tucker still wasn't in bed. She lurched up and looked at the clock: four forty-five. She should have felt relieved that she hadn't overslept. She didn't.

She groped on the floor for her robe, going into the bathroom to use the toilet and find the sweats he'd loaned her. They fit, but barely. No underwear, which might have felt weird if panic wasn't thrumming through her. She slid into her shoes and went out to the hallway. Shea's room was still unoccupied. Del paused outside the other closed doors but the rooms were quiet inside.

She went down the stairs, where a television flickered against the walls. Tucker was here, then. He probably couldn't sleep. She remembered his restlessness, how he used to wander the house at night.

She reached the bottom of the stairs, having already visually searched the living area for him. Someone came out of the kitchen, but the sight of Greer, and only Greer, killed her burgeoning relief. She forced a smile, looking behind him to the empty kitchen. "Hey. Where's Tucker?"

The way he tensed, the subtle tightening of his jaw . . .

"He left, didn't he?"

Greer's nod squeezed her chest.

"He wanted to get there early, get in position."

She stepped closer to him, having to look up into eyes like Tucker's. "No, he wanted to go without me. Because I don't have Darkness. Or—hopefully not—because I'm a girl and I can't fight."

He lifted a bare shoulder in a half shrug. "More the first one. There's something about Darkness you may not understand. It makes us . . . crazy to protect those we care about." One eyebrow arched. "I mean, those we *care* about."

Losing control scared Tucker. She remembered the fear in his eyes when he told the D'Rats about going nuts on Bengle.

"He left me behind because he cares about me?"

"Pretty much." He chewed his bottom lip, staring at the door. Ah, he wasn't happy about being left behind either.

"How about you? Are you still here because he cares about you?" she asked, hearing the snip in her voice.

"Pretty much," he said again. "Darius went with him, at least, so he's not alone. I get that he doesn't want them to know about us, but we stick together."

"Then let's go. We can't let them fight alone. What if there are more of the enemy, and they're outnumbered?"

She passed Greer and opened the front door—and remembered she had no car.

Tucker's car was in the drive. He'd come back! She searched the shadows inside the car but saw no sign of him.

"Darius drove."

She spun to find Greer standing right behind her, looking ready to restrain her, if necessary.

"You're a troublemaker." He narrowed his eyes. "Tucker'll have my head if I showed up with you. I've got the map, with the location marked. If he needs help, he'll buzz me." He pulled his cell phone out of his pocket. "I'm ready to go at a moment's notice. I know it's annoying, but we'll throw him off. Tucker has our best interests at heart." He obviously respected Tucker's order, even if he wasn't happy about it.

"I need to be part of this. Elgin has my mother. And I can help."

"You don't hold Darkness. How can you fight against two guys who do? Look, I know you're frustrated, maybe even pissed, but there's nothing you can do about it. I'm sure there's no point in suggesting you go back to bed. I'll make some coffee and you can beat on me if you want." His mouth quirked in a smile. "Cause you look like you want to do just that."

She took note of her posture—fists at her sides, mouth clenched—and took a deep breath. Giving up was not an option, nor was sitting around waiting. With her mother and Tucker in danger, she would *not* back down.

"Come on," he cajoled. "I make good coffee."

She put her hand on her tummy. "I couldn't drink anything. My stomach's all knotted up."

A map was open on the coffee table, and she wandered over. Foothills Road was circled. She visually traced it to where they were now, taking note of the highways and roads from one to the other.

Greer leaned close. "You don't want to walk there. It's a long way by foot, and who knows what dangerous creatures you might encounter on the way."

She pushed away from the map, releasing a ragged sigh.

"I can make something to eat, maybe some toast to settle your stomach."

She saw a key ring in a bowl by the front door and recognized the dice—Tucker's keys. Keys to the car that was sitting outside.

"You know, that sounds good. And coffee. I'm going to take a shower."

He gave her a nod and went into the kitchen as she headed to the base of the stairs. As soon as he was out of sight, she took two steps at a time, turned on the water, grabbed her purse, and then nearly tripped coming back down. She could hear the water coming down the pipes, so maybe that would buy her some time. She carefully lifted the keys, palming them so they didn't rattle together. Then she opened the door and slipped out.

Her heart was thudding in her chest like a playing card stuck in the spokes of a bicycle. She didn't dare look at the house, just kept her head down as she ran to the car. It was locked, and she didn't hit the button on his key fob, in case it beeped. She unlocked it, risking a glance to the front door—still closed—and got in.

She recited the roads that lead to Foothills as she drove, at first only vaguely aware of the feelings coming from the shifter. Once she got onto a highway, she could breathe again.

Do you want to know?

Yes, she did. She wrapped her hand over the leather shifter knob and sorted through a barrage of feelings, from their altercation with Elgin the night before to a powerful feeling of . . . protectiveness. And more. It knocked her back, and she realized her eyes weren't open, which was a really bad thing when you were driving eighty miles an hour down the highway.

She snapped to attention, and dammit, she couldn't keep her hand off the shifter. She was driving a manual transmission car, after all. She put her hand back, feeling that fierce protectiveness, along with the images Tucker had seen: her being thrown in the car, the car taking off, and then her falling out the passenger door. He'd freaked. Murderously, manically freaked inside, but he'd held it together to pull up beside her and help her into his car.

She shivered, pulling her hand and pressing it against her chest. That's what she would get if she stayed with him. Everything. More than everything. He scared her, but to be cared about, cherished like that, spoke to her at some deep level.

She passed the street she needed to turn down and had to go back. The front part of the neighborhood was sparsely populated. The back section was the newest, built during the boom when homes were overpriced. And oversized. She parked at the end of the first street.

She didn't have Darkness, but she had skills. She would stay hidden and look for an opportunity to help Tucker. Damned if she was going to sit by and let him deal with her mother's rescue without her.

TUCKER CREPT AROUND the buildings, alert for anything out of the ordinary. There were two unoccupied houses on one side of the street, a partially finished one on the other side. He moved stealthily, through the open rooms of that one, and then crossed the street to investigate the first finished one.

The sound of a car's engine halted him, and he peered around the front corner. A car was slowly coming down the street. Couldn't—shouldn't—be Darius. It was too early. Not that he could check his watch, but he hadn't been snooping long enough for it to be six. He thought it was the green Buick, but its lights were dark. When the passenger door opened, no interior light came on.

A shadow slinked from the car and across the yard to the second finished house on the street. Tucker felt a smile curve his snout, ducking down as the car continued up the side street.

When Tucker reemerged, he saw no sign of the shadow that lay in wait for him. Hunkering down, he stayed close to the bare concrete walls of the house until he reached the corner. Darkness seemed to camouflage the vibration they normally gave off, which could work for and against him.

He crossed the two lots between the houses, staying close to the clumps of weeds that grew in bunches here and there. The moon wasn't full but was bright enough to give him a sense of what was around. It would do. Because they weren't animals in a real sense, they didn't gain the fine-tuned senses animals possess.

The scrape of shoe against concrete stilled him for a moment before he continued on. Was it Elgin or his sidekick? Probably Bengle, so Elgin could roll in right on time and pretend to want to talk to his long-lost son.

The windows had been broken out, making the block home appear to have gaping eyes. Tucker melted into smoke, rolling into the opening and drifting up behind Bengle, whom he found crouched in human form by the front window. Perfect, one on one. Tucker went back to his wolf form. Bengle's head jerked toward him, probably catching the movement.

"What the—"

Tucker lunged at him, and Bengle Became in that instant, knocking him back. Tucker skidded across the concrete floor but was on his feet immediately. Good thing, too, because Bengle was flying at him, claws extended. As his name suggested, he'd chosen the form of a tiger. Tucker rolled as Bengle landed hard, then reared around and bit at his flank. He'd tussled with the son of a bitch before, knew to tear him apart bit by bit. Bengle fought harder this time, swatting Tucker and batting him aside.

He came back in time to take another chunk of Bengle's dark hide.

Bengle swiped and tore a piece of Tucker's substance this time. Yes, it did weaken him, though it would take a lot more of those to take him down. The two beasts circled, the lean wolf and the bulky tiger. Tucker was faster, dodging in, lunging, and getting out before Bengle could react.

Break him down, bit by bit, and then move in for the kill. Tucker could not let him get away this time. He had to take him down before Elgin returned.

Bengle jumped, landed on Tucker and sent him to the floor. Damn, he weighed a ton. Tucker reared up and took a chunk out of his stomach. The "flesh" had no taste, only a thick texture. It broke off in his mouth, and he spit it out and watched it disintegrate as Bengle screamed in some unholy voice and rolled over Tucker to back away.

Tucker grabbed him, but Bengle tossed him off—and came face to face with something not human and not distinctly any kind of beast.

Darius. *Hell.*

Darius wrapped his long arms around the tiger's neck while sliding his body beneath him. His legs came up around Bengle's body, and Darius face-planted into the tiger's throat.

Tucker staggered to his four feet and watched the bizarre sight. Darius looked more like a demon, though Tucker wasn't sure if that was by design or lack of training. He'd already been working with Darkness before Tucker had found him. That he'd chosen a form near human made sense; Darius could be man in Darkness, whole, able to use his legs.

Right now he was jeopardizing the whole takedown. The tiger could barely struggle with the leech attached to him, sucking out his substance. Finally, he became man again, and Darius crouched over him and twisted his neck. It cracked, echoing against the bare walls, followed by the thud of his head as he dropped to the floor.

Darius stood, rubbing his hands together, facing Tucker. His limbs looked long and rubbery, his hands huge. "Now that's how it's done."

Tucker remained in Darkness, uneasiness prickling through him. "You were supposed to stay in the car."

Darius's features were indistinct, even in the light, but Tucker could well imagine the smug look on his face when he said, "You weren't getting it done, Tucker. I could see you needed help."

"I had it under control."

"That's what you want to think. Maybe I should be the Alpha, huh?" He laughed, but he wasn't entirely joking.

"Get back in the car, before—"

The sound of a car's engine cut him short, and they both moved to the window and watched the Buick glide by. The soft sound of a chirp near his foot brought Tucker's attention to a cell phone near a duffel bag. Elgin's name lit the screen.

Darius grabbed it and answered before Tucker could stop him. "Yeah?"

"There are two cars in the area, neither one Tucker's—

or at least the one he was driving yesterday. Have you seen anything?"

"Nope."

Two cars? Tucker's heart hitched. He didn't want a couple of kids who were sneaking off to get high or laid stumbling into their situation.

"Maybe he brought some friends," Elgin said. "I'm going to check it out."

"I'll keep an eye on things here," Darius said.

The moment he disconnected, Tucker cuffed him. Darius clamped onto Tucker's arm, his whole body ready to attack.

"You're out of line," Tucker whispered. He hated that he couldn't depend on him to have his back. Tucker had only fought alone, never in a situation like this. He shook off his grip.

"You're not in charge of me. I do what I want." Darius took off into the night, as slick as mercury, in the direction Elgin had driven.

Chapter Thirteen

DEL CROUCHED INSIDE the unfinished house when she heard the car. The roof was open to the sky. Moonlight spilled into some of the rooms, casting shadows like bars from the skeleton-framed walls. The construction crew had only started the roof; several boards lay on top of the concrete walls, looking precarious.

She peered over the edge of the window opening and watched the car creep down the street. Was it the green Buick? It was hard to tell, though she could see the driver was on his cell phone by the square of light inside the car.

Something—or someone, she couldn't be sure—darted in front of the car, too close to be trying to hide. It ran toward the house where she was hunkering down. Tucker? Oh, no, he was leading Elgin right to her!

No, not Tucker—at least she didn't think so. She clearly saw a human-shaped shadow, though it ran in an unnatural lope across the dirt yard and into the door opening. One of them, then.

The car stopped in the road, and the driver got out. The interior light didn't go on, so she still couldn't see if it was Elgin. He evaporated, or probably Became, and in terror she watched his shadow moving toward the house, too.

Then, just behind him, another shadow. Wolf. Tucker. All heading toward her.

She slid from her spot and made to go around a narrow concrete wall to hide behind it. She came face-to-face with the man she'd seen first. Man, and yet . . . Darkness. He blinked in surprise at seeing her, then ducked and looked behind him at the sound of something scraping on the floor.

She ducked around the wall and found herself in the garage. He didn't follow, didn't try to grab her. Darius, maybe? She kept close to the wall as she headed to the opening at the front of the house where the garage door would go. She would be no help inside, where she could be grabbed and used as a hostage.

Where was Tucker?

She turned the corner and ran right into a hard, dark creature. Swallowing her scream, she stepped back, ready to fight. Tucker became man again, gripping her arms tight, his anger at her being there clear in what she could see of his face.

A scream of agony jerked their attention to the house. They ran to the first window, and then the second. He ducked back, pulling her with him. She pressed close as he peered around the edge.

The sight, at least what she could see of it, tightened her throat. One man standing, his hand held out as though to ward off someone. A glow, faint and blue, emanated from his hand. Elgin. Darius, in human form, too, writhed on the floor.

"Tucker, where's the girl? I know she's here somewhere."

Elgin thought Darius was Tucker. Darius was gasping in pain, unable to answer. What was he doing to him? Why couldn't Darius Become—and fight or run? Whatever Elgin was doing with his hand . . . he was using some supernatural weapon.

She could feel it, painful pulses, like the way being at a concert might feel, only the throbbing bass hurt. Could Elgin emit sound waves? She ducked back against the concrete wall, and it lessened. The concrete blocks acted like a buffer. She pulled Tucker back, too, gesturing to the wall. He nodded but dared another peek.

They had to help Darius.

Darius was panting now, dragging himself away from Elgin.

Elgin dropped his hand, and the painful waves stopped. He knelt down closer to Darius. "You're not Tucker. But you are my progeny. I can feel me in you. Don't try to Become, or I'll hit you with the Force again. It will stop you, and if I do it long enough, your cells will explode." Elgin said all this as though they were having a nice chat. "Where's Tucker? Give me his location and I'll spare you."

Tucker was wolf shadow again, having leaped to the

bare windowsill, his body compressed as he readied to leap.

"Right behind you, you son of a—"

Tucker hit, sending Elgin to the floor. Darius rolled out of the way just before he'd have gotten flattened.

"Grab hold of him," Tucker said as he fought to keep Elgin from turning over and freeing his hands.

Elgin Became, twisting and growling, slashing at Tucker with fangs. Darius grabbed for Elgin's thrashing hind legs.

Del climbed up on the sill, ready to jump down and help, if necessary. She knew better than to throw herself into the fray. Tucker's fangs tore at Elgin, shredding off bits of Darkness.

Elgin twisted, chomped down on Tucker's paw, and then lunged for his throat. It looked like blood pouring from Tucker's neck, like a real wound. *No!* Would it weaken him? Then Elgin used the trick she'd seen Tucker do during his show: he disappeared into mist. When he reappeared, he morphed back to man only a few feet in front of her, facing Tucker and Darius, who scrambled to their feet.

Elgin shot his hand out, dropping both men to their knees, stripping away their Darkness. The sound waves threw her backward, and she fell to the ground clutching her head. Once the brick wall was between them, though, she was able to try to get up. The waves churned her stomach, throbbed through her entire being.

They would explode her cells, he'd said. She believed it, too, holding her stomach as she tried to stand. Only when she was directly behind the wall could she even manage the strength to do it.

She heard Tucker's and Darius's groans of agony. No, she couldn't let Elgin kill them. She pulled herself up, ready for the blast again. Her heart plunged at the sight of Tucker struggling to get to his feet while curled in pain.

Have to . . . stop him.

She dropped down again, unable to bear it. How was Tucker even able to move under the direct onslaught? Her gaze locked onto the heavy boards on top of the walls, longer than her body, maybe a foot wide. From her vantage point, she could see the top of Elgin's head.

You can do it.

She concentrated on the boards, Elgin's head, the boards . . . the board shifted. Through the bricks, the sonic blast was muffled, but it still hurt all through her body. Her head. She clenched her jaw, teeth gnashing together, and focused all of her attention, her anger, and her fear into moving that damned board.

It flew off the wall and whacked Elgin exactly where she'd intended. The board fell to the floor, taking Elgin with it. Tucker slid down to his knees, his face pale. She only spared him a glance, though, her attention returning to Elgin as she climbed over the sill again. His body twitched, hands trembling, the board lying over his face. She searched for something else to use as a weapon.

He had taken her mother. Maybe even killed her. He'd tried to kill Tucker.

She grabbed a smaller board and approached him. He would never hurt her or anyone she loved again. Tucker staggered over to her, his breaths coming thick and heavy.

"Nails," he managed to say.

She looked at the board she was holding, then followed his nod to the one on top of Elgin. Two nail heads gleamed in the dull light. Tucker kicked the board while she held her weapon like a baseball bat, ready to strike.

Two huge nails pulled away from Elgin's forehead, out from the two huge holes they'd left in it. His eyes stared at nothing, his mouth open and moving, as though he were trying to say something. Blood trickled out as his body trembled again.

"Where's my mother?" she asked, leaning down into his face.

That mouth turned up into a macabre smile, and a breath hissed out of his mouth. No word, just a sound like air being released from a tire. His face went slack.

She shook his shoulders. "Where is she?" Hysteria crept into her voice. She could barely move him, her fingers curled into his shirt as she continued to try to shake him. His head lolled to the side.

Tucker's hand closed over her arm while the other hand checked his pulse. "He's dead."

"No."

He pulled her into his arms. "You saved us, Del."

"Son of a bitch!" That from Darius, who was trying to pull himself up to a sitting position. "I still can't Become. What the hell did he do to us?"

Anger tightened Tucker's voice as she felt him turn toward Darius. "You and I will talk later."

"The trunk!" She tore away from Tucker's embrace

and raced out to the car still parked in the road. "She might be in the trunk."

She heard his footsteps behind her as she pounded across the dirt and jerked the driver's door open. It was too dark to see the dashboard, so she groped and pulled on every lever and button until she heard the trunk pop open.

He was already back there, lifting the lid when she ran up next to him.

Empty. She nearly collapsed with disappointment. "I'll never find her. I'll never . . ."

He braced his hands on her shoulders, turning her to face him. His words were low and calm. "He took this car to where she is. You can find her."

"I can't . . . " Hope washed through her, and she nodded so hard it made her dizzy. "Yes. Yes, I can find her." She started touching the felt interior of the trunk.

Fear. Her mother's fear and discomfort and concern for Del. It blasted her nearly as strongly as Elgin's weapon. She ran to the driver's seat, dropping down in it and gripping the steering wheel.

Home. Where's home?

She saw a house, a yard, and felt the sense of the place. She turned the key in the ignition. "Get in. I think I can get to his house."

"Hey!"

They both turned to Darius, who'd dragged himself to the middle of the front yard.

"We can't leave him here," she said.

"Yes, we can," he said beneath his breath. "We'll be

back for you," he called to Darius. Then he got in and pulled the door shut. "Go."

She didn't hesitate, putting the car into gear and driving out of the subdivision. "What happened?"

"He went off the rails, no regard to the plan we had in place. Got all Alpha on me, thinking he should be in charge. I don't trust him enough to take him with us."

"No. We don't know what we're going to find. Or who lives with Elgin."

When she reached the Foothills entrance, she closed her eyes again, concentrating. She followed the sense of *home* several miles down the road and then onto another road. Signs announced *CAL ENERGY RESEARCH CO.* and another right behind it warned trespassers away.

She drove in through the open gate, spotting a large gray building up ahead. "It's an industrial building."

"Over there, see the smaller buildings? Maybe the employees live there."

"These are the people from the other dimension. The ones who would kill us if they knew we were here."

He surveyed the area. "Then we make damned sure they don't."

The sky behind the mountains was beginning to lighten. A few of the homes had lights on inside, signs of activity.

"He wouldn't have brought her here, would he?" She didn't want to think about what he might have done to her.

"She said she was going back to her people."

"But she'd broken the rules. They're not going to

just let her come back and live here like normal. They would . . ."

"We've got to start with Elgin's house. We'll find something there." He put his hand on her arm, his fingers closing gently around her. "You can find it, Del, if you concentrate."

And not freak out. "Okay." She took a deep breath, curling her fingers over the steering wheel, connecting to the thoughts and feelings it held. "Elgin was . . . he was angry at my mom. I can feel his anger, and the way he felt she was his. She betrayed him by leaving, and he couldn't handle that."

She focused on the house she'd seen. "They all look alike: neatly trimmed yards, arches over the front doors. How am I going to find his?"

Tucker pointed at the garage door opener on the visor. "I try every door until one opens."

She released a breath. "Good idea." Her relief was short-lived.

A man walked out of the house they were passing, his gaze on their car. His expression revealed his curiosity: why was Elgin coming home at six in the morning? The car's windows were dark, but were they dark enough?

"Hey, Elgin," the man called out. "Everything okay?" He paused, obviously expecting Elgin to lower the window and respond.

The garage door of the house next-door opened. She waved, hoping he could see that acknowledgment and nothing more. Tucker closed the door as soon as the car pulled inside.

"We don't have much time," he whispered, getting out. "If that guy thinks something's up, he'll be investigating. And if Elgin doesn't come to the door when he knocks, he'll definitely suspect something."

"Thanks for that reassuring thought." She passed him and reached for the door leading into the house.

He pushed her back, his hand on her collarbone. "Let me go first. I can tell if someone else is in there."

She nodded, and he went in, his chin tilted up as though he were sniffing the air. They passed through the kitchen, and she grabbed a knife from the butcher block on the counter. Not that it would be any defense against people who could use sonic weapons. Or Become. But she had her own weapon: Tucker. Could he Become, though?

The house looked like any normal, suburban ranch-style home, devoid of personal touches. She had to remember that these people were human, at least at their core. They'd been passing as regular humans for a long time now. Carrie had told her that they had willed their bodies to take on a conventional human look when they'd first come here.

Tucker stopped in front of the hallway and gave her an affirmative look. Someone else was in the house, probably in one of the bedrooms. He held out his hand, and she saw Darkness at the edges. His ability was coming back. He continued, taking slow, deliberate steps until he reached the first door, which was open. She peered around the doorway, her body pressed near his.

It was an office, dark and unoccupied. They moved on

to the next room, which was nearly empty. The last door was closed.

Tucker gave her a somber nod. Whoever was in the house . . . that's where they were. Elgin's wife? Roommate? Or her mother.

Her insides were wound so tightly she could hardly breathe. Tucker shimmered in Darkness, ready for anything. He reached for the knob, turned it, and pushed it open.

"Mom!" The sight of her, tied to the bedposts, weakened Del's knees.

Tucker checked the room and the closet as Del raced to Carrie's side. She took inventory, her mom alive—tired but alive—her shoulders bare above the sheets . . . naked? No, she didn't want to think about what that meant.

"Del! What . . . how . . ."

While Carrie had been gawking at Del, Tucker had cut her free on that side of the bed with his claws.

"We have to get you out of here, Mom." Del used the knife to cut the ropes on her side. "I'll tell you everything later."

"Elgin. He was going to . . ." She looked at Tucker, and Del saw gratitude and relief. "I didn't mean to tell him about you, Tucker. I'm so sorry."

"Don't worry about me. Or Elgin. He's dead. But right now we're in the middle of an enclave of your people."

Carrie grabbed the sheets as she got up. Tucker took note. "I'll be in the hallway."

Del helped her to her feet, searching for her clothes.

They were piled in the corner. "Here, hold onto the dresser." She planted Carrie's hands on the corner and grabbed the clothes, then helped her put them on.

"I'm so weak. My legs feel rubbery," Carrie said.

"It's okay. We'll help you out."

Her mom leaned on her as they stepped into the hallway. Tucker took them in, and without hesitating, scooped her up in his arms. "Let's get to the car."

Carrie held onto Tucker's shoulder, though her body was stiff with her discomfort. If Tucker noticed, he didn't let on, intent on getting to the garage. Del got into the back seat with her mother, and Tucker got into the driver's side. He waited until they were settled in before opening the garage door. The neighbor was heading up the walkway to the front door.

Tucker backed out, then calmly pulled away, sending the garage door closing as he left. He opened the window a few inches and waved back at the man who was standing there watching.

More people were out and starting their day. Of course, everybody here would know everybody else—worse than a small town. Hopefully it wouldn't look strange to see Elgin's car out and about so early.

Carrie was sitting up now, gripping Del's hand as she watched, clearly expecting to be stopped. Her eyes were wide, bloodshot. What she'd gone through . . . Del pulled her close and pressed her head against her shoulder, hoping to block the view of their surroundings.

When they pulled through the entrance, Carrie let

out a small sob, then gripped Del. "He didn't hurt you, did he?"

Del should be asking that question, but she merely shook her head. "I'm fine. Tucker took good care of me, kept me safe." She met his gaze in the rearview mirror, but he shifted it away, focusing on the road ahead.

"I have to go back to the Foothills for Darius."

If Tucker had regained his Darkness, Darius should have, too. When they drove back, Darius was pulling himself along the road, his face slick with sweat, biceps bulging with the strain. He glared as Tucker pulled up beside him.

Tucker lowered the window. "Try Becoming."

Darius's glare softened, and he turned first to a black mist and then to the human shape she'd seen earlier. Interesting that he'd chosen that form. He was tall, strong . . . whole again. Carrie's grip tightened, and she screamed.

"It's okay, Mom. Darius is with us. He's one of the offspring."

Darius leaned into the open driver's window and jabbed his finger at Tucker. "I will kick your ass for leaving me like that."

"Later," Tucker said through gritted teeth. "I need you to take care of Elgin and Bengle. Put them in here; run them out to the desert. The longer they go without being found, the better."

"Still giving orders," Darius growled.

"I'm asking you. I've got to get them home." Tucker looked at Del. "How did you get here?"

"I stole your car. It's parked a couple of streets up."

He turned back to Darius. "Get in. Please." The word was soaked in a patronizing tone. "We'll drive to my car, then you can take this one."

Darius waited long enough that she thought he might refuse. Finally, he stalked around the front and got in.

Carrie whimpered, burying her head against Del's shoulder, her whole body stiffening. Darius looked frightening, his body and face a dark mass of that quicksilver smoke.

Darius looked back at them but turned to Tucker as he pulled down the street. "Dammit, Tucker, you left me there in a heap."

"I couldn't afford to bring you along. You were acting recklessly."

She directed Tucker to his car, and he stopped beside it. "I'll see you back at the house," he told Darius in a voice that said they would definitely have a talk. She wanted to know exactly what had happened, but now wasn't the time to ask. They got out, and Darius slid over to the driver's seat.

Del wanted to sit up front with Tucker, to hold his hand, to feel him. But she needed to be with her mom, who was still trembling, so she crammed into the small back seat with her.

Del met Tucker's gaze again, and he said, "I'm going to take you to your car, Del. You need to get her home."

She nodded, then held her mom as she listened to Tucker call Greer and give him a rundown of what had happened, thus enlightening her and her mom as well. Thankfully, he left out the details. Carrie didn't need to know any of that, only that she was safe from Elgin. That they all were.

"You put Greer in a tight spot, Del," Tucker said. "Once he figured out you were gone, he started heading our way. But I made him promise to stay put."

"Tell him I'm sorry. No, I'll tell him. But dammit, Tuck, this was my problem. It wasn't right leaving you to deal with it while I sat around waiting for you to not get killed."

It took awhile for Carrie to calm down again. Del was glad she'd never seen Tucker Become, but it wouldn't matter. Carrie would only see him as a man with Darkness, a beast, and something to fear.

Tucker knew that. She could see it in the shadows of his eyes when she caught him watching her. He always looked away before she could hold that silver gaze.

It felt like forever had passed since they'd last been in that parking garage. So much had changed since then. As Tucker helped her out of the car, and her mother shied away from his hand, she saw that nothing had changed. His eyes were as shuttered as they had been the day before.

"Wait," she told him, and helped her mom into her car. He was leaning against his car, staring at the concrete floor. She returned to him. "Tuck, I want to talk to you. Later, when my mom is settled in."

Soft agony drenched his eyes. "There's nothing to talk about. Go back to your life, Del."

Without him. That's what he was saying.

She grabbed onto his hand. "I'm sorry I turned away

from you all those years ago. I needed time to assimilate everything, and by then you were gone. I'm not going to turn away from you again."

He shook his head. "Then I'm turning away from you. Your mother is never going to feel comfortable around me, and I don't blame her. Especially now. She'll always look at me like she did Darius. Like you did back in my bedroom," he said in a lower voice.

"You were testing me, and I failed. But only in that moment, because I wasn't prepared. Admit it; you wanted me to flinch, to show fear."

"Yeah, I did. Then I could finally put you in my past and move on."

"Did it work?"

His mouth twisted in a chagrined smile. "No. You'll be just as hard to walk away from now as you were then. Harder."

She took his face in her hands. "You hold Darkness, but you are not Darkness. What I see when I look at you is what you are: a man. A man who deserves love. *My* love, as a matter of fact, and I don't give that to just anybody. In fact, Tuck, I haven't given my heart to anyone but you. Mom accused me of comparing any guy who was interested in me to you. She was right. Not because you're gorgeous or haunted or a bad boy." She slid her hand down over his heart, splaying her fingers wide. "You're a good man. No matter what you hold, that's what I know. And here's what else I know: I'm not going anywhere, because I think you love me, too."

He held on for a second, and she could see his turmoil: give in or keep his distance and protect her from his dark nature.

"Kiss her, Tucker."

They both looked up to see her mom inside the car, the window now open.

"She's been sad and lonely ever since you left. That was my fault, because I saw my husband in you. But you're not Elgin. And my heart ached, too, because I loved you like a son. So kiss her, love her, and make her happy. She deserves that, too." She rolled up the window and sat back in the passenger seat, turning away to give them privacy. Del had mistaken the expression on her face. Not fear but grief for the decisions she'd made.

She and Tucker looked at each other in surprise.

"Now it's only your own wall to overcome," she said, moving close to him, her hand cupping his cheek.

He leaned down and kissed her, softly, slowly. "Clearly I'm not good at putting up a wall between us. You broke it down the moment you said you needed me. When you looked into my eyes, and I could see everything you felt for me . . . damn, Del, I was lost."

She leaned up and kissed his chin. "You don't ever have to be lost again. I'll always be here."

Read on for a sneak peek
at the next exciting installment of Jaime Rush's
***Offspring* series,**

Darkness Becomes Her,

Coming in June 2012
from Avon Books

Prologue

Fifteen years earlier

"Wake up, Ally!"

Her daddy's voice, hands shaking her. Not a dream. Her eyes snapped open, finding his face, scared and desperate, hovering in front of her.

"You've got to hide now."

She tumbled out of bed, heart squeezing her chest. "What's happening, Daddy?"

"The man I told you might hurt me, he's here, Ally-bean."

She swiped up her penguin, the one with the special coin sewn inside it. She couldn't breathe all of a sudden. "Where's Mommy?"

"She's all right. He won't hurt her."

"But he'll hurt me?" The words squeaked out of her mouth.

"I don't know what he'll do. I just want to make sure you're safe."

He tugged her down the hall to the closet and shoved aside the coats.

"How will I know when it's safe to come out?" Fear made her voice a whisper.

"Either your mother or I will come get you. You'll be okay."

He didn't look as though he felt that way, and that made her even more scared.

"I love you, Allybean." And he closed the door, shutting her in the dark.

Daddy had always seemed overprotective and kind of worried. When she turned nine a year ago, he told her there was a man who wanted to hurt him: his own brother, Russell. Daddy had shown her a picture, trained her to be on the lookout for him. He had something called the Darkness inside him. Daddy had promised to tell her more when she was old enough to understand.

Now Russell was here, and she didn't understand, not at all. Minutes dragged by, each one so long, so painful. She squeezed her penguin and felt the coin her father had put inside. Through the fur, she could barely make out the raised cross on it. The symbol was supposed to protect her, to hide her presence from the man who was hunting Daddy.

A *thump* froze her. Like someone being thrown against the wall. Loud, harsh voices, two men . . . and Mommy. They were screaming all at once, their words crashing on top of each other. Another *thump.* Tears filled her eyes. *Please, don't die, Daddy.*

She tried to peer through the slats in the bifold door but could only see the hallway. What if she crawled out but kept the penguin with her? It would only be for a few seconds.

Her mom cried out, the same way she did when she dropped a heavy pan on her foot last year.

Mommy!

The men's voices got even louder, but nothing from her mommy. Her ears were buzzing, making it hard to hear more than angry voices. *Have to look.*

She stretched through the opening. What she saw froze her heart. There was blood everywhere, splattered on the walls and puddling on the floor. And her mommy, she was lying on the floor. Not moving. Ally stifled a cry.

"I can heal her," one of the men said in a voice so thick it was impossible to tell who was talking. "I can use Darkness to heal her, but then she'll have it, too."

"Don't touch her."

Those words, raw and hoarse.

The men moved into view, like two boxers, squaring off, punching, lunging like in the movies Daddy watched. She was in the dark, and she was pretty sure they couldn't see her. They fought, growling and shoving, moving in and out of her view.

The bad man said, "Does the child have Darkness, too?"

"No, she's normal. Leave her out of this."

The child? *Her.*

"My son inherited it," Russell said. "Your daughter probably did, too. If she holds Darkness, she'll have to be . . . contained. Trained."

"The hell she does!" A loud sound, and a chair slid across the floor.

She'd stretched farther out into the hallway without even realizing it, and now saw Russell, his back to her, his foot on her father's chest. She wanted to burst out and save him but stopped herself. Anger and fear, it froze her, closing in her vision. No, not her vision. She saw blackness. Her father, turning into . . . she blinked. Couldn't be. He was now a black blob of smoke.

Russell stepped back, facing the dark mist. "You've been trying to suppress Darkness, just like before. But I've been working with it, mastering it."

He became the same smoke. The blobs took shape, changing to something solid again, to huge, mean wolves. Her daddy's wolf was gray, Russell's was black. The wolves fought, snarling, and then the black wolf spun like the Tasmanian Devil in the cartoons and wrapped itself around her father's wolf. Terror gripped her, making her eyes water and her throat dry. Was she really seeing this?

Go back in!

The shadows became men again, and one of them fell to the floor. The bad man! Her daddy was okay!

She got to her feet. Her legs felt so wobbly, and she hardly had breath. She took a staggering step toward the kitchen, her fingers clutching the penguin. Her daddy knelt by her mommy's body on the floor. "No. You can't be gone." Such pain in his words. Smoke snaked out of his hands as he leaned over her, sending . . . sending the smoke into her mommy.

"No!" The word roared out of her throat.

He turned to her and . . . his eyes were gray, not the green she knew. He wasn't her daddy. He looked like him, but she knew, knew in her heart, that he wasn't. Russell had gone into her daddy's body.

"There you are." He jumped up and grabbed for her.

Chapter One

"What are you on to, checking up on me?" Lachlan narrowed his eyes as his brother sauntered into the kitchen.

Magnus managed to find a reason to come to the family's remote estate, dubbed Sanctuary, every few days for some lame reason or another. As usual, he surveyed the house, checking to see, perhaps, if garbage was piling up or if Lachlan had painted any of the walls black.

Magnus poured himself a cup of tea from the pot sitting on the counter, then opened the fridge to pull out milk and frowned. "If I *were* checking up on you, I'd point out the lack of quality food in the fridge." He closed the door and tugged on Lachlan's hair. "Or that you haven't cut your hair in months; it's as long as a girl's." Magnus pinched Lachlan's chin. "At least you shave, but next time use a mirror. You missed some spots."

"Considering you and the clerks at the stores are the

only people I see, I have no need for a cut and style." Lachlan stroked the strip of hair that ran from the bottom of his lower lip to his beard. "I was bored, figured I'd try something different."

Magnus lifted the back of Lachlan's old T-shirt. "No lash marks on your back, at least. Saw a movie about those monks who beat themselves with whips in punishment."

Lachlan shoved him away, not that the big guy moved much. "Sod off. Thought you were busy, as you're so happy to tell me, living life, shagging women, and making up for lost time. Why are you driving all the way out here to check up on me? Making sure I haven't gone over the edge?"

Magnus dropped down into a chair and propped his big black shoes on the kitchen table. "Holing up here by yourself day in and day out, it's bound to make you mad. You're a pain in my arse, but you're all the family I got. You want to live like a monk, keep punishing yourself for the past, nothing I can do about that. But I don't want to come out and find your rotting body."

Lachlan smirked. "I didn't know you cared."

"I'm the one who's going to have to deal with it."

Lachlan leaned against the counter. "Ah, it's the cleanup you're worried about. I promise you, I'll not be doing myself in. That's a coward's way out. I'll live till I'm a hundred and deserve every wretched minute of it. Now you can move on."

Magnus tilted his head. "I do care. It's me and you, Locky. That's all we've got."

"Don't remind me, Maggie." Not that he could forget why their parents were dead.

"You're the only one who hates yourself, you know. It's time to ease up."

"'Ease up'? I killed our mum, for God's sake. Would have killed you, too, if I hadn't come to my senses. I'd hate me, if I were you."

"You made a mistake, a big one, but you had no idea that the outcome would be as horrific as it was. It's been almost a year, Locky."

Lachlan kept his expression passive. He didn't deserve forgiveness or release. Or the childhood nickname. "I'm happy working on my projects, being alone, and living vicariously through your exploits. Get any gigs?"

Magnus gave him an exasperated sigh, hopefully giving up on him. "I'm filling in for an ailing drummer Saturday for the Wee Willies. And I've got a date. Not that you'd know what one of those is."

"I know what a bloody date is."

Magnus's laugh came out a low rumble. "Oh, that's right, you learned all about that kind of thing in those chat rooms and from watching dirty movies." When Lachlan narrowed his eyes, Magnus raised his hands. "I'm not judging you. I watched them, too. We were hot-blooded teenage boys living a life in isolated areas, being home schooled. We had to get our jollies somewhere. But we're not boys anymore, not being hunted down. It's time to go out in the world and live." He raised a thick eyebrow. "And touch women."

"I've no interest in either. I'll stick to my cars, thank you."

Magnus nodded toward the newspaper on the table.

"At least you're keeping up with society. The girl I'm seeing, she's in there. Front page of the Living section." When Lachlan didn't move toward the paper, Magnus said, "Go on, have a peek."

She must be a number if he was eager to show her off. Or he was really hot for her. Maybe both. His brother always filled Lachlan in on the girl he was dating, a different one every time. Not to brag, but probably out of an attempt to draw him out into the world. Tempt him.

Dutifully, Lachlan turned to the section. The story featured a winter carnival to raise money for a local girl who not only had muscular dystrophy but had recently undergone a bone marrow transplant. An anonymous marrow donor had saved her life, but medical bills threatened to bury the family.

There, in the background of a photo of people setting up booths, was a petite, dark-haired woman, her shiny hair in a pixie cut that fanned over her shoulders. Unaware of the camera, she held up a large sign while two people hammered it in place. Her profile showed apple cheeks, tight-fitting jeans, and a sweater that molded a great set of knockers.

"Nice," he allowed.

"I haven't even pointed her out yet." Magnus jabbed his finger at the same woman. "Name's Jessie. I've fallen for her."

"That's what you said about the last four or five. Or ten."

Magnus's mouth turned up in a roguish smile. "Yeah, and I did, temporarily."

"What happens after you've fallen? You just get up? That's it, the feelings are all done?"

"Yeah, like the bubbles going out of a soda after it's been sitting for a while. But there's something about Jessie that I can't put my finger on."

"Well, she's hot."

"She is, but that's not it. Dunno. Anyway, you could come to the carnival—"

"No, thanks. Have fun with your girl. I hope you're using a condom."

Magnus smirked the same way he had. "I didn't know *you* cared."

"I was thinking of the lass, you horn dog. 'Twould serve you right, catching crabs or lobsters or whatever."

Instead of taking the bait, Magnus laughed, shaking his curls. Well, sure, he could be in a good mood. He was going to get laid.

Magnus pushed to his feet. "All right, carry on with your wallowing. Might help your mood if you got laid, too."

"Stop reading my mind. Invasive, meddling—"

Magnus chuckled as he headed to the front door. "Nice job on the fifty-five, by the way. Sexy as hell. I'd say the sixteen coats of Marine Spar varnish did the trick." He let the door close behind him.

Lachlan knew that '55 Chevy truck was as sexy as his life was going to get. He carried the mugs to the sink but stopped short. The shiny, bloodred tile backsplash was wobbling. The floor shifted under his feet. Earthquake? He set the mugs on the counter, and the house started spinning. He grabbed onto the back of a chair at the small table, but it gave way. So did he.

Not the house, him. He broke out in a cold sweat, his body rigid. *Stroke? Heart attack?* Those words pinged through his head and seized his chest as he shivered on the tile floor. Then he was standing in a completely different place. He saw a Ferris wheel, booths, but everything was blurred. Over there, someone in the near distance. He stumbled toward him but his gaze went to the mound on the ground: Magnus, dead. Somehow, he knew his brother was dead. Standing next to him was a woman, petite . . . the woman in the photograph? No one else, just the two of them.

Then he snapped back to the kitchen, staring at the can lights in the ceiling. He patted his hands down his body. Here, alive. He got to his feet and grabbed the newspaper. Yes, the same woman. He slumped to the chair, feeling the same peculiar fatigue wash through him that he used to get after he astral-projected. Except he couldn't astral-project anymore. He'd lost that ability when his father had tried to save his sanity.

The carnival, that's what he'd seen. He grabbed his phone and called Magnus. "Get back here. Now."

Magnus walked in a few minutes later, concern in his eyes. For a second he reminded Lachlan of their mother. They'd both gotten her brown eyes, but only Magnus had her curls. A sharp pain stabbed him at the thought of her.

Magnus dropped into the chair next to Lachlan's. "What's up? I just left and you looked fine. Well, as fine as you can look. Now you look like shite."

"Something happened. I think I astral-projected." With shaking hands, he held out the newspaper, pointing to the lass. "She's going to kill you."

"What the devil are you talking about?"

Lachlan told him what had happened.

"You're serious?"

"You think I'd make something like this up?"

"You saw her kill me?" Not a small dose of skepticism in Magnus's voice.

"I saw her standing over you after she'd killed you."

"You were only able to project to the present and past. So you're telling me your ability's come back, and now you can see the future?"

"I'm telling you what I saw. So unless that's happened in the past, then yes, I saw the future."

Magnus dropped the paper on the table. "You haven't had a glimmer of your abilities in ten months, and now, the moment I show you a picture of a girl I want to start seeing—"

"You think I'm making this up—or imagining it—because I'm *jealous* that you're interested in someone?" He rammed his fingers back through his hair, tangling in the strands. Yeah, a bit too long.

"It's either that or you're going mad again, in which case I hope it is jealousy. Jessie's sweet, shy, and she's not coming on to me. The opposite, in fact, which is probably why I'm so fascinated by her. So if she's a homicidal woman who picked me for her next victim, she's not doing a great job of luring me in."

"Maybe she is doing a great job. Play hard to get. Just

like you said, that only makes you want her more. You don't think smart women know that will snag a play-around like you?"

Magnus rolled his eyes. "Why would she want to kill me? Do you know how many female serial killers there have been in history? Like, a handful. I hate to say it, but it's much more likely that it's your imagination. We don't know what the side effects of the antidote might be. It was something Dad worried about."

Was he going crazy again? What he'd felt when he saw Magnus dead . . . it shattered him. He couldn't take a chance that this wasn't real.

"It happened—it's going to happen—at the carnival. Are you planning to be there with her?"

"I'm helping her with last minute details tonight."

"Did she bat her eyes at you, tell you how much work there was to do, so little time to finish it?"

Magnus narrowed his eyes. "I offered all on my own, no eye-batting necessary."

"What do you know about her?"

"She just moved here, got a job at the music shop where I bought my kit. She won't let me pay for her coffee or lunch, yet I know she's tight on money because she wanted a large latte but settled for the small. She's volunteering her time at this carnival because someone in her life had muscular dystrophy. You can tell it means something to her when she talks about it. She's warm and playful with the kids who take classes. And you forget, if she had any murderous thoughts, I'd probably pick up on them."

Magnus could read thoughts, or at least pick up words here or there. He hadn't lost his abilities when he'd taken the antidote. Lachlan had been bitter about that, but he'd come to realize he didn't deserve abilities, not when he'd killed someone by using them. Now, though, something *had* come back. Something different than what he'd had.

"I'll go back earlier and see what happened." He had always been able to project at will, but nothing happened.

"So it's not back, then," Magnus said a minute later. "You haven't gone all tense and twitchy."

Lachlan's eyes snapped open. "Humor me and stay away from the carnival."

"How did she kill me in this supposed vision? Knife in the parlor? Candlestick in the drawing room."

"Sure, joke around when I'm telling you your life is in danger. I couldn't tell how you'd died, only that you were dead. Everything around you was a blur, but I didn't see anyone else."

"Give me more, Locky."

Frustration swamped him. "I don't have any more."

Magnus got up and walked to the foyer.

Lachlan followed. "I never hallucinated. That wasn't what happened with mum."

"You saw something that wasn't there. By definition, that's a hallucination." He pushed open the door and turned back. "Last time you thought you had everything under control, and then you lost it. Don't do anything crazy."

Magnus left, and Lachlan stalked back to the table, staring at the picture of the girl. He had to find out more about her. He'd lost both his mother and father in the last eleven months. He wasn't about to lose his brother, not when he could prevent it. He could never live with himself if he didn't do something. Hopefully, Magnus wasn't in danger. But that meant his own sanity was.

Lachlan grabbed up the newspaper and walked to his room. The house was a square, like a fort, wrapped around a courtyard flourishing with flora, fauna, and fungus, his father's fascinations. The trek from one place in the house to another gave Lachlan too much time to think. He sat at the computer, booted it up, and waited through the process.

He'd been cut off from the world for so long, exposed to television more than to actual people. For the first half of his life his father had rented isolated homes. During the last half, they'd lived here in a house they owned, built in the middle of a large tract of land. Their social interactions consisted of brief forays into town.

Magnus made friends easily. He longed for the world, for contact. Lachlan had inherited the lack of need for others from his father. Dad could spend all day in his lab or out with the fungus. Lachlan did that with the old truck now, immersing himself in the process of restoring it. He'd done it several times before, resurrecting something old, rusty, and broken into something whole.

Something he could never do with himself.

He launched into a search for Jessie Bellandre, finding several mentions. One was a blog entry dated two years earlier in which her name appeared. The blogger was a sixteen-year-old with muscular dystrophy, talking about her experience at an MDA summer camp. Her counselor was Jessie, and the picture of the woman in a canoe matched the Jessie in the article, except she had blond, wavy hair. The camp was in Iowa.

After several more false leads, he found her again, this time in Nevada six months ago. Again, involved in a Muscular Dystrophy Association function. So she definitely had a connection with the disease. But what was the connection to the horror he'd seen? Why was she moving around the country so often, changing her looks? He kept digging.

He found three older mentions, all in the Boston area. In the two pictures, she had dark, long hair. At some point she started moving around and changing her looks. Why?

Given an age in one of the articles, he dug deeper and found something alarming: eleven years ago Jessie Bellandre, aged fourteen, died from a fatal form of muscular dystrophy. Someone had made a tribute page to honor children who had passed on, trying to drum up sympathy and donations. There was no picture. He went through several steps of finding the woman who'd put up the page. She no longer maintained it, having moved on to other projects, and all she could tell him about Jessie was that she had been a foster child, thus the lack of a picture.

Stymied, Lachlan stared at the tribute listing and then at the picture of her in the paper. They were the same age, or would have been. Both had lived in Boston. Now this Jessie—Magnus's Jessie—had been resurrected as a woman who was clearly living a lie.

He grabbed his cell phone to call Magnus, but stopped. His brother would say it was a coincidence, even though it wasn't a common name, and that he was stretching things to match his crazy scenario. He needed more. He was going to have to hunt her down.

Chapter Two

Whenever Lachlan ventured out into the world, he felt like a vampire, pretending to be like the others he walked among. Jessie's current residence wasn't listed in the phone directory, but he had a piece of insider information: he knew where she worked.

He walked into the store located in Annapolis, Maryland. It was damned hard not to seek her out the moment the door closed behind him and appear only mildly curious. No woman in sight. Bells dinged against the glass. The bittersweet sound of a violin flowed from somewhere in the back.

A man walked out and asked if he needed help.

Yeah, tell me what you know about the girl working for you.

"Just browsing."

"I'm Glen, if you need anything."

Lachlan gave the man a nod and wandered over to an

impressive display of electric guitars mounted on the far wall.

Her voice reached out to him, like a ribbon wrapping sinuously around his stomach. It was soft and sweet and full of her smile. He could tell even before he saw her.

"Look, you brought tears to my eyes, Charles. That was incredible."

Lachlan turned and felt a trip in his heartbeat at the sight of her. She was walking from the back with another woman and her young son, who was holding a violin case and beaming with pride. Smitten, too, judging by the way he looked at Jessie.

Her eyes were misty, all right. She knelt down to his level. "When you're a famous superstar, will you still remember the girl at the music store?"

The boy laughed and gave her a quick hug.

"Yeah, she has that effect on most of the males who come in here."

Lachlan turned to Glen, startled to see that the man was talking to him. Lachlan was about to deny the smitten part but laughed it off instead. He pretended to peruse the drum kits displayed in front of a wall of mirrors. Between the electric guitars that hung over them, he could watch her reflection. She was even prettier in person, her eyes glowing with sincerity and admiration. She wore slim black pants that outlined a luscious figure and a black top with grunge-style ruffles.

She died eleven years ago.

Or was pretending to be someone else. Either way, combined with what he'd seen in his projection, he didn't like it, despite her innocent appearance. Likely, it was all a show, along with playing hard to get.

He shifted his attention away as she began to look up. He imagined Magnus sitting behind the blue kit, as he had for the last few years at the Sanctuary, banging away in the basement. Curls bouncing wildly as he moved the sticks so fast they were a blur. Bliss on his face. Once, Lachlan had tried his hand at it, when no one else was around. Good thing, too, he thought now, as he had not a speck of rhythm.

He caught his own reflection in the mirror. Holy hell, was that him? His hair was long and mussed, button-down shirt hanging loose over faded jeans with a square, ragged hole in one knee. He hadn't looked at himself for a while, had avoided mirrors. Now he saw a stranger staring back at him.

"I'm going home for lunch," Jessie said, leaning behind the counter and pulling out an enormous dark purple bag. She glanced his way, their gazes locking in the reflection for a second. She paused for just as long before turning away and leaving.

The trick was to leave right behind her without looking as though he was following. He reached for the tag on the brass cymbal, noticing the calluses on his hands.

"I know your type," a man right behind him said.

Lachlan turned to face Glen, surprised to see a smile and not an accusation.

"Lives for the music, stays up all night playing the songs in his head. That was me, before the wife and kids and shop." He gestured to the place in general.

"You've pegged me, dreaming on my lunch break." Lachlan glanced at his watch. "Which, unfortunately, is over."

He knew she'd gone to the right, and spotted her as she turned the corner at the end of the block. Lucky break, that. He jogged down the sidewalk, slowing as he took the same corner. She got into a big SUV, and hearing the locks snick as he passed by, he again fought the urge to look at her. He got into his truck, which did looked damned good, though he still saw all the things that needed to be done yet.

Lachlan didn't take the time to revel in the purr of the engine, the only real pleasure he allowed himself. He was too busy watching the rear of Jessie's black Yukon as he followed her into an apartment complex some ten minutes later. He parked several spaces away and observed her jump down from the vehicle and take the stairs two at a time. She disappeared into unit 14B on the second floor.

Lachlan knew he would find the answers in her apartment. He tried to astral-project to her apartment but once again failed. Had the projection been a tease? His imagination? The thought tightened his chest. The picture of Jessie triggered the projection last time, but now that he was near her, he couldn't get it to work. He'd have to break in the old-fashioned way. He had done it before, every time his dad locked himself out of his lab, sometimes leaving not only his key in there but the backups as well.

Jessie remained inside long enough to eat lunch and then reemerged. He could understand why Magnus was smitten with her. Her hips moved eloquently as she walked to her vehicle. Interestingly, she scanned the parking lot, not paranoid exactly, but wary. When she drove off, Lachlan remained.

He carried a toolbox and appeared to be looking for an address. After knocking on her door, he identified himself as the handyman she'd called and pretended to converse with her through the door.

"The dispatcher said you can't get the door to open . . . Okay, no worries, I'll get you out of there."

He worked on the lock with the pick kit. When he opened the door, he continued the "conversation" as though she stood right there inviting him in to work on the knob.

The apartment was small and sparse, with generic furniture. Coupons littered the two-seater kitchen table's surface, each cut in a neat square and stacked in categories like food and household items. Several magazines lay on the counter, one open to a recipe for buttermilk biscuits. The one on top had the address square cut away. A To Do list had several bullet-point items scribbled all over it.

In the small living area, a sewing kit sat by the recliner, lid open to reveal spools of thread and a red heart-shaped pincushion. Juxtaposing the domestic ambience, a stack of well-read love novels on the end table sported covers with couples in provocative poses. So she liked the steamy stuff, eh?

Even further from the norm, a gymnast's mat filled a corner, a punching bag hanging above it. Several DVDs on karate were stacked by the television. Bars and a fine steel mesh reinforced the windows.

Ah, now he was getting somewhere. Someone had drawn a cross on the wall, four lines and a small circle in the middle. He looked around more closely. At the bottom of the stack of novels he found a hard-bound notebook, ragged with use. Sketches of demonic beings filled the pages, each identified as creatures like werewolves and shapeshifters. Many had X's through them. He took pictures of a few pages with his cell phone, then one of the cross.

He took a few steps into the only bedroom. Not a lot of personal effects here either. A framed picture, fuzzy blanket, a small stuffed penguin on the made bed that looked like it had seen years in the clutches of a child. The sight of it stabbed him in the chest for some reason. He saw no other signs of a child living here, so it had to be hers. He took a picture of that, too.

A key slid into the lock at the front door. Lachlan stepped out of view, watching as she dashed into the kitchen and grabbed some papers on the counter. The vision flashed through his mind again, this woman standing over his brother's body, and he reacted. He crossed the few feet, catching her eye with the movement, but he already had his arms around her waist before she could get in a kick. She pitched all her weight forward, throwing him off balance enough that she wriggled free. She spun, with a roundhouse kick to his side. Pain exploded, making him grunt. He regained his balance, finding her bouncing on her feet, fists raised, ready to attack.

Both fear and anger blazed in eyes a rich blend of green and chocolate. No sign of that sweetness now. A ruse, as he'd expected. She jabbed, and when he backed up, kicked. He grabbed her foot and sent her stumbling backward. She twisted, slamming sideways into him using karate moves she no doubt practiced on that mat. She was strong, and it hurt. It also felt good in a strange way.

He grabbed her arms, clamping them against her sides. She swiveled, shoving him against the wall and, with that split second of freedom, made to run toward the door. He grabbed her shoulder and yanked her back, intending to pin her against him. She twisted her ankle and pushed his foot enough to send him to the floor, her along with him. They crashed, both taking the brunt of the fall. His arms locked around her.

They ended up with her on top, her back plastered to his front. As she struggled to free herself, her ass ground against his pelvis. Of all damned things, the movement shot heat through him. This was a fight, not sex. But he was thinking about sex, which was crazy.

She brought her elbow down, but he blocked before she could dig the point into his side. He was too breathless to talk, too focused on winning. She shoved her hip sideways and kicked his leg, shooting pain up the length of it. This time she was able to roll to the side and gain her footing, jumping to her feet. He was right behind her and grabbed her again.

He shoved her against the wall, hearing her breath whoosh out of her. Didn't matter; she made to ram her knee into his groin. She was a fighter, and a practiced one at that. She hadn't hesitated to fight him. He used his body to hold her to the wall, grabbing her flailing arms and anchoring them at her head level. Their heavy breathing was synchronized, and with each breath, their bodies pressed tighter together. Her breasts, soft and round, nipples hardened, sent heat pulsing through him.

Bloody fine time for that.

She wriggled again, aiming a deadly look at him. The look didn't kill him, but it heightened the heat. He had the insane urge to grind into her but held himself in check. What the hell was wrong with him? He'd numbed himself to anything sensual, any desire, and here he felt it with this potentially homicidal woman.

She tried one last time to jerk up her knee, and his pelvis mashed even harder against her. Good God, he felt an erection, the first one since—

"I won't be an easy rape, you son of a bitch," she spat out at him, still breathless. "Is this what Russell's doing now, sending crazed rapists after me?"

Rape? Of course, his wayward cock. "I'm not going to rape you. I want to know why you're going to kill my brother, Magnus."

She blinked in confusion. "Magnus? *Kill him?* Are you crazy? I have no intentions of *killing* him."

"I am a little crazy, actually. I saw a vision of the future, you standing over his body." No need to go into any more than that.

"You saw a vision. As in a crystal ball type vision?"

"Don't look at *me* like I'm the strange one. You're obviously into some weird stuff. What's the symbol mean?" He nodded toward the sort of cross. "Are you a devil worshiper?"

Her laugh was hoarse. "No."

"Why didn't you scream for help, even when you thought I was a rapist? What are you hiding?"

Something happened. One moment they were there, him pressing her against the wall, and the next all he saw was a black blur and then he was thrown across the room. He hit the wall and slid to the floor. He blinked, stumbling to his feet even though every muscle in his body screamed in pain.

She stood where she'd been, eyes wide and mouth trembling. "Get out of here. I would never hurt Magnus. Just get out of here."

The energy in the room had changed, sparking and electric. She was scared of whatever had happened.

Lachlan rubbed his shoulder. "What did you do to me?"

"Get out."

Or she'd do it again? No, she hadn't exactly said it as a threat. Still, it was a threat nonetheless. He glanced at the symbol and then at her. Her hands were clenched into fists at her sides. Now her whole body shook, as though she might explode. She took deep breaths, making her chest rise and fall.

He walked out, watching her the whole time. He had astral-projected into many different places and time periods, into battles and even one of the Holocaust camps. He had never felt this kind of energy.

She *was* dangerous. He got into his truck and drove directly to Magnus's new flat.

JESSIE STOOD IN her apartment for a long time, letting the trembles rumble through her body. Everything that had just happened washed across her mind, pulsing like a strobe. Fear of dying, of being raped, and then the bizarreness of the man's accusation. He had triggered her Darkness, which scared her as much as anything else.

She took a deep breath and looked around for the papers she'd come back for. They were all over the floor. It hurt to bend down and grab them, and she winced. *Wince all you want now, because you can't when you get back to work.*

She walked outside, pausing on the landing to make sure the man was gone. No sign of him. She hadn't screamed. Couldn't scream. The last thing she needed was having the police dig too deeply into her life. She walked to her Yukon, taking calming breaths.

Her phone was beeping, signifying that someone had triggered her security alarm. She might have known the jerk was waiting for her if she'd taken her phone with her. She was tempted to click on the link, but there wasn't enough time. A cluster of charms hung from her rearview mirror: an angel, rabbit's foot, horseshoe, four-leaf clover encased in plastic, and a Star of David, and they dangled back and forth as she maneuvered through traffic.

A quick fix of her face, a brush through her hair, and she looked as normal as she had when she left.

Glen looked up when she walked in. "Must have been a hectic lunch break," he said with a smile.

Damn, not exactly as normal. "Had to fit in a lot of errands."

"If you need a couple of minutes to defrazzle, go ahead and take them. I know you've got a busy weekend."

Glen and his wife Toni were great bosses, and even better people. The Tripps ran the store together. She was their only employee, running the storefront, handling calls and paperwork. She was good with numbers. They were stable, dependable, and impersonal. She liked working in small businesses where her employers wouldn't be bothered as much by her erratic work history. That also meant settling for menial jobs that didn't pay much.

Toni and the two grade-school Tripps came rushing in at mid-afternoon, as they did every weekday.

"Hey, Jessie!" the girls called as they gushed with enviable energy and innocence, dropping their backpacks on the floor. "Carnival's tomorrow!"

Toni rolled her eyes as she picked up the packs, as she did every day, and set them behind the curved desk where Jessie worked.

"Yep! You gonna ride the scary rides?" Jessie asked, bending down to their level.

"Will you ride with us?"

"Sure."

Both girls giggled and exchanged looks. "We might

throw up, though," they said in unison, more like twins than girls who were two years apart.

"Ewww!" Jessie said, pinching her nose. "Then definitely do not ride the scary rides. I'd be tossing my cookies right along with you."

The girls commenced to making barfing noises until Toni shushed them. She set them on their homework just off the main desk. Jessie watched them asking their mom for help and felt a lump in her chest even as she smiled. When she was their age, she'd had a mom and dad, too. Thank God they didn't know how tenuous life can be, how all that matters can be ripped away in minutes.

Five other children came in for guitar lessons, and Jessie entertained them until class started. For a few minutes no one was in the front room. Glen was in the repair shop in back and no customers wandered in. Her head still felt light, as though she hadn't eaten for hours. She logged into the security software and clicked on the link for her system. It recorded any activity once it was triggered.

Her throat tightened at the sight of the man—Magnus's brother—walking into her apartment. He wasn't even creeping or sneaking, just walked in like he owned the place. Bastard. He looked around, taking pictures of a couple of pages in her notebook, walking to the doorway of her bedroom but not walking in.

The video quality wasn't good enough to see fine details. She realized she'd hoped to see his face again. He had dark, thick hair that fell past his shoulders and brown eyes with an exotic slant to them. He was good-looking, yeah, even though she felt pretty stupid thinking of him that way when he'd broken into her home and manhandled her.

Where have I seen him before? Oh, yeah, here! Right before she'd dashed home for lunch. He was stalking her! Her gaze went to the collection of signed pictures on the back wall. She remembered thinking he looked like one of those rockers from the eighties that Glen was so into, like Kip from Winger. The jerk probably followed her home.

Her attention went back to the monitor. She knew the moment the intruder heard her unlock the door; he ducked inside her bedroom doorway and waited for her. Even though she knew what would happen, watching it was odd, surreal, and scary. She didn't have this security system the last time she'd gotten a surprise visit.

She watched their fight. *I fought pretty damned good. Not good enough, though.*

He pinned her with his body, and she could feel all that muscle and hardness again, crushing her. Especially *that* hardness, which had thrown her, because she'd thought for sure he was connected to Russell, and the man's erection signified a different threat.

But he wasn't there for that. *Thank you, God.*

She glanced around to make sure no one had come in; she was engrossed enough to have missed it. Then she turned back to the screen. As her fear and anger had heightened, a smoky aura formed around her. But . . . there was something around *him*, too; not smoky, but a blurry form.

What the heck?

She paused the frame. Even studying him she couldn't make it out. That nothing else had the same blur meant it was attached to him. Either he also had Darkness, or he was some other kind of weird. No matter, he was bad news.

Her abilities had taken the man off-guard. If he, or Magnus, were working with Russell, they would have been prepared. She would be dead. The supposed brother claimed he'd had a vision of her killing Magnus. That was all he seemed concerned about, wanting to know why.

When she continued the video, it hit her: she would see her Darkness for the first time. She steeled herself as she watched the black mass that threw him across the room. *Me, but not me. It just took over; I had no control over it.* She shivered and closed the program. What if the whole seeing-a-vision thing was true? Darkness could kill. Could she?

She picked up her cell phone and called Magnus. *Please let me go to voice mail.*

Relief when his deep voice said, "'Lo, this is Magnus's phone. I hate that I missed your call. Don't make me hunt through the call log. Leave a message." Both men had a Scottish brogue to their voices. Magnus had told her he was born in the U.S. but got the brogue from his Scottish mother.

"Hi, it's Jessie," she said. "You're off the hook for tonight. I don't need any help with the carnival, and . . . I can't see you socially anymore. My life is too complicated in ways I can't explain. Take care of yourself."

Her mouth stretched into a frown. It wasn't like they'd done more than chat at the store, have a cup of coffee, and meet for lunch once. He'd kissed her cheek when he walked her back to the music store and said goodbye. She'd had the sense that he wanted to kiss her on the mouth, though, as his lips had lingered against her skin for a few moments. He probably would have, if the sensible part of her hadn't made her turn at the last second. She'd wanted the kiss, because she wanted to feel like the women in the romance novels she devoured, just for a little while . . .

You knew better. Why bother starting a flirtation when you're going to have to back away if it goes any further? Russell's going to find you eventually. You're either going to die or run again. No place for a man in that mess of a life.

Yeah . . . complicated. With a sigh, she deleted Magnus's number from her contacts list.

About the Author

Since she was a kid, JAIME RUSH has devoured books on unexplained mysteries and psychic phenomena. She *knew* she would be published, marry a fabulous guy, and win a Toyota Supra. Missing the romance, relationship drama, and action of her favorite television shows—*X-Files*, *Roswell*, and *Highlander*—she created her own mix in the *Offspring* series.

Jaime loves to hear from readers (unless they're deranged or don't have something nice to say). You can reach her at PO Box 10622, Naples, Florida, or through her website at *www.jaimerush.com*.